Come for Me

Southern Nights: Enigma 1

Ella Sheridan

Anita —
Enjoy the heat!
Ella Sheridan

Also by Ella Sheridan

Southern Nights
Teach Me
Trust Me
Take Me

Southern Nights: Enigma
Come for Me
Deceive Me
Destroy Me

If Only
Only for the Weekend
Only for the Night
Only for the Moment

Secrets
Unavailable
Undisclosed
Unshakable

∞

For news on Ella's new releases, free book opportunities, and more, sign up for her monthly newsletter at ellasheridanauthor.com.

Copyright

Praise for Southern Nights

Teach Me

"Chock full of violence, suspense, sex, and romance. *Teach Me* never stops moving forward, which makes it very difficult to put down, each chapter leaving you ready for the next."

— Hines & Bigham's Literary Tryst

"Emotionally gripping and an absolutely brilliant story. The writing was flawless and I found myself immersed in the entire plot from page one to the end."

— Cocktails and Books

Trust Me

"*Trust Me* should come with a warning of lost sleep and deep circles under your eyes, because that's what's going to happen once you start reading this riveting, suspenseful tale of love and revenge. You won't be able to sleep until you have reached the very last page."

— Sizzling Hot Book Reviews

"Boldly flavored writing, dynamic characters, and an insidious suspenseful plot will keep readers on the edge of their seats."

— Smexy Books

Take Me

"Solid plots, easy flowing dialogue between the characters and really yummy alpha males! That right there is the recipe for an awesome romance novel! Ella Sheridan has written a series that drew me in from the beginning and made me beg (harass?) her for more!"

— Blogging by Lisa

"I FREAKIN LOVED THIS BOOK! Chemistry so thick and heavy it will choke you, heartbreak so intense it will gut you, fear so severe it will take you to your knees."

— Bookworm Betties

Dedication

To Dain, who showed me what being completely in love really means. And to Livie, strong enough to stand alone, strong enough to surrender.

Thank you both for sharing your story with me.

Chapter One

The sight of Olivia's empty pillow registered as soon as Dain's eyes opened, but not its meaning. His wife never got up before he did—years in the military had assured he awoke at dawn no matter how much or how little sleep he'd gotten the night before. He usually stirred when the room was still dim, the weight of Livie's slight body half lying on his right side, the warm, sleepy scent of her filling his nose. His gift. His heaven after too many years of nothing of his own. His arms ached without her in them.

Where was she?

She'd been up for a while too; the scent of coffee lingered in the air, which meant it'd had time to drift from the kitchen into their bedroom. Running a hand across the bed found her side already cool.

Why wasn't she still in bed with him?

The sound of water running caught his attention, filtering through the closed door of their connecting bathroom. She was already in the shower.

Something was wrong.

Every instinct he'd honed in his forty-two years screamed at him to get to her. Senses alert for any alarm, he slipped from the bed and stalked across the room to the closed bathroom door. A moment listening revealed nothing but the flow of water.

Frustration and worry tangled together in his throat.

"Livie?"

Wet air slapped his face as he stepped into the daylit bathroom, but not until he saw Livie behind the glass shower door, head tilted back, eyes closed, did he take a full breath. Leaning against the wall, he watched as she lifted her hands to the mass of strawberry-blonde hair on her head, now water darkened and soapy. She slid her fingers through the strands as the water rinsed suds down her body. Damn, he'd never get tired of that body. Ten years of marriage hadn't lessened his desire for her a single iota. Livie had the pale cream complexion of a true Irishwoman, her smooth skin drawing his gaze down a long, slender neck to rounded breasts with plump nipples he could spend hours sucking and pulling. Her stomach was softly curved, her hips rounded like the bottom half of an hourglass, her legs long. At five-seven she still only came to his shoulder—a perfect fit, in his opinion. And when he imagined those curves against him, those legs dragging him closer between her thighs…

He dropped a hand to his naked cock and stroked, enjoying the hardening rush that seized his body.

Livie turned, opened her eyes. One green, one brown. Those beautiful mismatched eyes rested on his hand, his erection. A laugh bubbled from her full lips.

"Good morning, husband."

He slid his hand to the very tip and squeezed as he watched the water lovingly trace her body. "It certainly is now, wife."

When he lifted his shoulder from the doorjamb and began a slow stalk across the room, Livie shivered. Considering the light drift of steam in the room, he didn't think it was a chill causing that reaction. He stared, silent, branding her with every step, until the glass between them was moved aside and he joined her in the shower. Livie swallowed hard as she moved back to give him room. He kept pushing forward until her sweet body was trapped between his much bigger one and the wet shower wall.

The water was cooler than he'd expected—not cold, but not hot. Livie loved a hot shower. He frowned, settling his hands on her hips to keep her exactly where he wanted her. "What's wrong?"

It was more command than question, but Livie only looked puzzled. "Nothing's wrong. Why?"

He bent until his mouth came even with hers. Livie tried to push up on her toes, to bring their lips together, but he held tight, refusing her impulse. A sharp nip on her full bottom lip startled her.

"Why are you up?"

A shy, sly look blossomed in her eyes. "Is that what this is about? You're upset because I got out of bed without you? I am completely capable of managing a morning on my own, you know."

Of course he knew. She managed all the time when one of his security jobs for JCL required an overnight stay to protect a client. Just not when he was actually here.

"Don't try that snow job on me, wife," he growled. "Something's up. You can't distract me from finding out what."

"I can't?" Since he refused to let her lift enough to meet his lips, she leaned forward, her tongue landing on one tiny, already hard nipple. His groan echoed against the tile walls. When her teeth joined the dance, he abandoned the argument in favor of pulling her tight against him. The move allowed him just enough room to land a smack on one plump ass cheek.

Livie squeaked into his skin.

"I know I'm gonna have to punish you for leaving me all alone in that enormous bed. Do I also need to punish you for lying to me?"

A light laugh tickled the hollow below his collarbone. "Sounds fun."

He leaned back, searching out those mismatched eyes. She couldn't hide anything from him when he looked into her eyes. "Tell me, Olivia. Are you okay?"

Her eyes shared the smile that curved her wide mouth. "I'm okay. Really." She pushed up on tiptoe again, and this time he loosened his hold enough to allow it. "Just a little insomnia, that's all. You know these end-of-the-month hassles. But that's nothing to worry about. I'm fine."

Livie worked in accounting at a local Atlanta company, and yes, sometimes the final days of the month were a pain in the ass. Still…

Livie closed the distance between them, bringing her mouth to his, open and hot. Her hard nipples dragged through the rough hair on his chest, drawing moans from both of them. "You said something about a punishment?"

He eased back, ignoring her pout in favor of torturing her. "Turn around."

His wife turned the torture right around on him, shifting her body little by little, giving him the best view of all her delectable parts before finally facing the wall.

"Hands up."

She placed her palms on the cool tile, fingers spread. The rise and fall of her back quickened, matching his racing breaths.

"Tilt back, Livie. Give me that ass."

Livie lifted first one foot, then the other—about shoulder-width apart, equal distance from the wall. He gave one smooth inner thigh a smack. "Wider."

She spread for him. When she angled against the wall, her ass lifted and spread. His mouth watered at the sight of his beautiful wife ready and waiting for anything he wanted to give her. There was still so much he wanted to give her, always. He'd never be able to give her enough.

He palmed both ass cheeks. A rough massage had her lifting onto her toes.

"Dain!"

The first slap left a white print on her skin that quickly turned pink. Dain enjoyed the delicate jiggle of the plump swell before moving to the other.

Slap.

Livie moaned. So did he.

Setting up a slow rhythm, Dain savored the sight of his wife's surrender. Outside the bedroom, Livie knew how to take control, how to lead, and did often, especially at work. She wouldn't be the VP of Georgia Financial's accounting department otherwise. But here, with him, she gave exactly what they both needed—her body completely open to him, her pleasure his to provide, her love so palpable he could touch it, taste it, wrap himself in it. In her. His hand landed one last time on her perfect ass, and then he dropped to his knees behind her, bringing his lips to her fiery skin, skimming along the heat as he sought the wetness he knew awaited him between her legs.

And oh, was she wet.

He slid between arousal-swollen lips to finger her clit. When he stroked his tongue along her flaming ass, Livie jumped. "Please, Dain…oh God!"

The final word slid up an octave as he penetrated her with two thick fingers. Livie always felt too tight, like she would strangle him the minute he got inside her. It took a few strokes to open her up, to get to the point where he could thrust without fear of spilling himself immediately, thoroughly, in the snug depths of her body. This time he let his fingers stretch her, using the moment to savor the heat of her skin and the soft shivers his lips evoked as he kissed and licked and nipped her firm, rounded ass.

His ass. His wife. His Livie.

His whole world.

She pushed back against him, seeking her own pleasure and his, urging him to stand and take her. His teeth caught the under curve of one cheek, nipping hard as he delivered a last smack to the opposite side.

"Oh!"

Grinning, he stood up behind her, gripped her hips, and drew her backward until her back was almost flat, until those beautiful breasts dangled at the perfect angle for his hands, until her full ass was cuddled right against his aching cock. Until she was exactly how he wanted her. And then he bent over that sleek back.

His lips traced the furrow of her spine as he cupped her breasts. When he tugged at the erect nipples, he swore she flinched. "Okay?" he asked, pausing.

With a moan Livie arched into his hands. "I'm okay. Just a little tender."

A quick calculation told him she was close to her period. Knowing that, he took his time, teasing and pinching and tugging lightly, gentling her to the sensations. Only when her ass was grinding against him did he let himself get rough, just the way she usually liked for him to touch her.

"I could do this forever, wife," he whispered into the skin of her shoulder before gripping the slim line of muscle with his teeth, lining himself up, and sliding all the way inside her. He stopped hilt-deep, a growl rumbling up in his chest as he struggled to keep control, to make this last as long as he could bear for it to. If he'd had any choice, he'd never leave Livie's body. And from the way she not only accepted him but opened herself, her body clutching at his rock-hard cock as if she never wanted to let go, he knew she felt the same.

"Are you stuck?" she asked, breathless amusement underlying the words.

He ground in a circle inside her. "Maybe. Would you mind?"

"Hell no." She groaned as his cock stroked her deep inside. "But I'd really like to come sometime today."

"You would?" He chuckled, the act bumping his cockhead against her cervix. "Well, I live to serve."

"Yes, you do," she agreed sweetly as he began to thrust. And then the two of them were lost in the rhythm of advance and withdraw, in and out, over and over and over again until it felt like not only their bodies but their souls were one. Finally, unable to wait any longer, Dain pinched a nipple and Livie's clit at the same time, setting off a detonation that sucked him into oblivion with her.

When he came back to awareness, Livie was sagged against the shower wall, her smile wide and sated. Slipping his arms around her, he drew her up until they were back to chest. "Now that is a good morning, wife."

"The kind only you can give," Livie told him, nuzzling underneath his chin. One hand lifted to run along the side of his head, just beneath the edge of his Mohawk. "You need to shave before work."

And there it was, damn reality creeping in. Dain sighed. "Right."

There was still time for a little play as he washed her body, then his. When they exited the shower together, he was hard again and Livie was chuckling at his predicament. "That's what you get for messing around before work."

"You could come take care of it for me, wife."

"I could." She wrapped a towel around her naked body and headed for the bedroom. "Unfortunately you picked a morning when I have a meeting. Sorry!"

"Tease," he called after her, but his lips curled into a smile as he turned to the sink to shave. "You better make up for that when you get home tonight!"

Chapter Two

Olivia's body continued to hum an hour later despite the fact that the only thing protecting her from the chill of the patient room in which she waited was a thin paper gown. She hadn't lied to Dain; she did have a meeting, just not at work. With her doctor. She hadn't wanted him to worry—when Dain worried, he drove her absolutely crazy. She was already worried enough for the both of them, and maybe a dozen more controlling husbands besides.

When the door to her room opened with a peremptory knock, her heart jumped into her throat.

"Morning, Olivia."

"Maryann." Olivia and Dr. Maryann Paton had graduated from Emory University together. They'd been friends before they became doctor and patient, and Maryann knew her well. When Maryann's assessing gaze ran over Olivia, she couldn't help shifting on the paper cover sticking to her thighs and butt.

"Nervous?"

Olivia tried to read into her friend's tone but couldn't. "Of course I am. I know something's not right; otherwise I wouldn't be here, for God's sake."

Maryann turned to set Olivia's file on the small counter in the room, and Olivia swore she saw a smile tugging at her friend's lips. That was good, right? She couldn't be dying of cancer or something if her friend was smiling.

The tension in her muscles doubled as Maryann turned to face her. Her friend chuckled when their eyes met. "Relax, girlfriend. I've got you."

Olivia tried, she really did, but until she knew what was going on... Her mind sought the memory of this morning, of Dain's strong arms supporting her, holding her close. She pulled that strength around her now, wishing contrarily that she'd told him about this meeting and had him here in the room with her for real. "Would you please just get on with it before I shake out of my skin?"

Maryann sat on the tiny wheeled stool and slid it close to Olivia, placing a chilly hand on her bare knee. "Okay, ready?"

Olivia searched Maryann's intent eyes. "Yes."

A sharp nod, then, "You're pregnant."

Olivia sucked in air so fast she choked on it. "What?"

The word was more strangled sound than an actual question, but Maryann got the gist of the meaning. "You're pregnant!" She shouted the words this time, standing quickly and throwing her arms around Olivia's shoulders. "It finally happened, my friend! You're going to have a baby."

"But... What..." Olivia searched her brain, but only jumbles of questions and emotions surfaced. "How...?"

Maryann quirked an eyebrow up. "With that stud of a husband, do you really have to ask how this happened?"

That did draw a smile, however small—Dain was a stud, no doubt about it, and fertile enough to impregnate a woman at fifty paces. Just not *her*. "I thought..."

Maryann shrugged. "I thought so too. All the tests certainly indicated that this was unlikely. But if I've learned anything in this practice, it's that miracles happen." She paused, staring deep into Livie's eyes. "Are you okay with this? What about Dain?"

"Oh, Dain will be ecstatic." They'd wanted a child since they married ten years ago, but after years of trying and testing and the strain of treatments, they'd given up. They had each other, Dain had told her. That was enough. And so they'd built their life around each other and no additions except Dain's team. He treated the men and women he worked with like family, sort of a replacement for the children they couldn't share. Some small part of her had never been able to give up the dream, though, even when science and common sense told her it was impossible. And now…

Good God.

"Maryann, what about… I mean, I'm too old for this, aren't I?"

"You're only thirty-nine, Olivia. Women are having children later and later. We'll keep a close eye on you, but there's nothing to indicate that you can't carry and deliver this baby just fine. Your hormone levels are perfect. I'll be doing some extra blood work to make sure it stays that way, be sure you're progressing like you should. Get you started on prenatal vitamins. But"—she waved a hand toward Olivia's file on the counter—"you couldn't be more textbook at the moment. Olivia…" Maryann hugged her again, her tight clasp somehow reassuring Olivia in a way nothing else could. "You're doing this. You're going to be fine, and so will this baby." She leaned back, a huge grin on her face. "Dain is gonna freak."

"You know he will." And finally, thinking about her husband's reaction, a real, full smile took over her lips. "He really will." She shook her head. "I'm having a baby."

"You are."

And then Olivia was on her feet, paper gown floating around her as she and Maryann shared a total girlie moment of hopping around the room clutching at each other and squealing out their joy.

She was still riding the high when she arrived at the office a little while later. All the way up to the fourth floor, she considered ways to tell Dain her news. She'd given up having a moment like this years ago; surely there was a way to make it special. But it had to be tonight. She'd never keep a secret from Dain longer than a few hours—he knew her too well, not to mention he was in the business of secrets. Working at JCL Security, he handled client safety, investigated cases, did security reviews—the man knew his stuff, and he certainly read her well enough to know when his wife wasn't telling him something. She'd almost told him this morning in the shower, when she'd flinched from his touch. Her breasts had become so sensitive; she just hadn't made a connection between the sensation and pregnancy, not when she'd thought it was an impossibility for her. Overactive hormones, maybe, or something else, like cancer or some kind of disease, yes. Never pregnancy.

Her hand fluttered down to her still-flat belly as the elevator doors slid open. No, definitely not pregnancy, but oh God, how fantastic was this little miracle?

She stepped out of the elevator when it arrived at the top floor. Would their baby take after her or Dain? Her husband was exotic, half-Caucasian, half-African American, a beautiful blend with his dark bronze skin and near-black hair and eyes. He had sharp features that only added to the intimidation of his thick muscles and the Mohawk that curved along his head. Would a son look like him? What about a daughter? Olivia's grandmother had migrated from Ireland, passing down her Irish looks to each generation. Would Olivia do the same? Or would their child blend the two cultures somehow? As she pushed open one of the glass doors leading into Georgia Financial, the possibilities whirled in her head. Could she wait till tonight to talk to Dain? Maybe she could call and see if he was busy for lunch.

She didn't notice the quiet until she was well into the office. Usually an hour into the workday the place was bustling; despite what people thought about accountants, her team was a lively bunch. But silence met her as she entered. Rosie's desk, right up front, stood empty, and beyond the half wall that separated the receptionist from what they'd dubbed "cubicle land," nothing moved. No Felicia charging back and forth between desks. No Stan popping up to yell questions across the room. No…anyone.

"Stan?" Olivia called. "Rosie?"

Anyone?

Walking farther into the room, she found desk after desk unoccupied, all looking like they'd been left in a rush. A big rush. On Stan's desk, the phone lay half-on, half-off the cradle, and…was that blood?

She leaned closer, holding her breath. A bright red streak trailed from the white surface of the phone to the pad of paper on Stan's desk. Blood, definitely blood.

Olivia jerked up. Her height enabled her to just barely see over the cubicle walls. The three conference rooms to the right, all with floor-to-ceiling glass separating them from the main room, were empty. The back contained individual offices, including hers, but the blinds were drawn in each one. Uncertain what to do, she shoved a hand down into her purse, searching frantically for her cell phone as she moved cautiously toward her office.

She made it to the final cubicle before jerking to a stop.

She'd found Stan.

Olivia shrank back behind the cubicle wall closest to her, the sight seared on the backs of her eyelids as she clamped them tight. Shaking sobs piled up behind her closed lips. He was dead. Stan was dead. If she'd had any doubt, the wide-open, glassy eyes would've erased them. A large red stain had spread across the left side of his chest, the pocket protector they teased him about so often a mangled mess in his pocket. His body lay, limp, crumpled against the back wall of the room, blocking the path to the hallway leading to the utility and break areas of their company suite. What carpet his body didn't cover, the blood did.

God, so much blood.

Her mouth flooded with saliva. *Not now, baby. Let's keep it down, okay?*

She glanced around the wall one more time, hoping, praying. But no, Stan was definitely dead. Who would do such a thing? And where was everyone else?

You can't wait around to find out, wife.

Dain's voice in her head calmed her shaking and the gasping breaths she hadn't quite been able to get ahold of. Pivoting toward the glass doors she'd entered so innocently mere moments ago, she forced one foot in front of the other, trying desperately to think, to reason, to answer the million questions screaming through her brain, but…nothing. All she could do was rush for the door.

She'd reached the first cubicle, the one belonging to their new intern, John David, when the sound of a door slamming jerked her to a halt.

"Just shut the fuck up!"

Instinct had Olivia dropping to a crouch in the small space next to John David's chair. The zipper of her purse resisted her efforts to jerk it open, get to her phone. Tears stung the backs of her eyes.

Down the hall that led to the CEO's office, she swore she heard the sounds of a fight. Punches— there was no mistaking the impact of something hard on someone's bone, or the agonizing groan of true pain. One foot slid backward, then the other, retreating from the threat, pulling Olivia toward the back of the room silently, without thought.

And then that same angry voice. A man's voice. "I don't give a shit what you want! You got us into this mess. Tie them up now, or I'll make sure you join your friend out there. You won't go as quick as he did though, Cecil; I promise you that."

Cecil? Georgia Financial's CEO, Cecil Derrick? What did he have to do with all this?

"But…please wait. Please! I—"

The distinct sound of a gun cocking echoed down the hall. Everything inside Olivia went tight at that quiet click. She knew it so well; Dain had made sure she trained regularly with a gun despite the fact that she didn't carry. What would an accountant need with a handgun, right?

Apparently a lot, Olivia, at least today.

Cecil's response was lost in the pounding of her heartbeat in her ears. A cubicle edge digging into her spine urged her to turn, to watch where she was going, to hurry. Run.

Run.

How much time did she have? The men's arguing filtered from the hall. Were they coming closer? Her office was in the far corner of the main room, the door locked, keys in her purse. Eyeing the distance to her office door, she tried to gauge how much time it would take to cross the open yards of floor, unlock her door, and get inside before anyone saw her.

Too much time. Next to her office was the sales manager's, René, and next to his, their public relations officer, Carla. Both closed tight.

Think, Livie. Think hard.

She needed a weapon. A place to hide.

The stubborn zipper of her purse finally yielded to a hard jerk. Thank God. Searching fingers found her cell phone in the side pocket. Clutching the slender case like the lifeline it was, she eased around the wall hiding her and crept the few feet to Stan's body, struggling to hold back the whimper that rose to her lips.

It seemed to take forever to step over him. She couldn't avoid the blood, but she wiped her shoes on the carpet just past the body—how could her friend be the body?—hoping a trail wouldn't lead the man with the gun right to her. She could think of that, think of where she needed to go, but she couldn't think as she lifted her phone and started to dial. She pulled up Dain's cell phone automatically, knowing that wasn't the number she should call, knowing he wouldn't answer his cell while he was at work, but the message didn't seem to communicate to her fingers. Finally she gave up, hit Call, and brought the phone to her ear. Ringing blasted her, loud in the silence, as she crept down the hall that somehow seemed far more sinister for all the bright fluorescent lights illuminating the way.

"This is Dain. Leave a message. Unless you're Livie; then come find me, wife. You know what I'm waiting for."

The message had begun as a joke the first year of their marriage. Dain had told her he didn't want to talk to her on the phone; he wanted to hold her in his arms, kiss her senseless, and then take her over and over until neither one of them could talk. One day she'd dialed his number, only to have that same voice message greet her. It had been there ever since, every time she called. Sometimes she called just to hear it, in fact. This time, though, tears of frustration pricked her eyes.

She managed to wait for the beep without giving in to hysteria.

"Dain?" His name came out shaky, and all she could think was that he'd be worried, then do something stupid like charge to the rescue. Which she wanted desperately, but she wouldn't risk him. He'd given her enough basic training to find weapons around her, hide, stay safe. That's all she had to do, stay safe until help came.

Clearing her throat, she forced her next words to be steady. "Dain, there's something wrong here."

The door to the employee kitchen/break room came into view, just up and to the right. She crossed her fingers as the other hand tightened on her phone. "Stan's— Stan's dead. There's blood." God, what did she need to tell him that would help? She was fumbling around in the dark as much as she was in the harshly lit hallway. "I can't find everyone else. I'm going to the kitchen. I'm in the kitchen, okay?" He'd understand that. Lots of weapons to protect herself with in a kitchen.

She needed to get to the kitchen, get off the phone. She had to call the police. But though her feet kept moving, she didn't want to let go of Dain, even if all she could get of him was his voice mail. "I've got to go. I'll call your office after I call the cops, okay? I'm all right. I am…"

And that's when she remembered it wasn't just her here, creeping down the hall, trying to stay safe. It was her and their baby. A baby she might never get a chance to tell Dain about in person.

She had to keep their baby alive. But first, "Dain? Listen, I need to tell you, just in case. I know I'll be fine, but just in case…" *Stop repeating yourself, Livie.* "Dain, I'm pregnant. Do you understand? I'm pregnant, husband." Her voice went soft on the nickname even as she laid a hand flat on the cool surface of the kitchen door. "I'm having our baby, so you come get me, damn it. Come get us." A scared, shaky sigh escaped. "I love you, Dain."

She clicked End, took a deep breath, and shoved the door open in front of her.

Chapter Three

"Tap out, stupid bastard."

"Tap out's for sissies," Saint wheezed. Considering Dain had the man's shoulder pressed into his carotid, cutting off blood flow, getting out a single recognizable word would be amazing—three was a fucking miracle.

"Ten seconds, Saint," Elliot said nearby, warning the man how much time he had before he was likely to black out. "Nine. Eight. Seven. Six. Five—"

King swore from the other side of the mat. "Saint!"

Without warning Dain's captive flipped his long legs into the air, his spine bending in ways that would seem impossible with his neck immobile. But he had the length in his torso to manage. In a blink his knees were on either side of Dain's head and his calves were locked at Dain's nape. Before Dain could duck his head to slip out of the hold, Saint flung him over his long body, loosening his legs at the end to keep from breaking Dain's neck.

"One!" Elliot yelled as Dain's back slammed into the mat. With a quick kippup, Saint's massive weight landed on top of him, crushing the air from his lungs without warning.

"Goddamn." It was Dain's turn to wheeze.

"Dain!"

The yell from the workout room door brought all their heads up except Dain's, stuck beneath one of Saint's bony knees.

"Code Red," Jack Quinn called. There was no hesitation in their response; all four team members were on their feet and running for the door in seconds.

"Where's the party?" Dain yelled as they raced after his boss down the hall toward one of the conference rooms. Jack shook his head but didn't answer, causing Dain's heartbeat to pick up speed. Jack Quinn was the head of JCL Security, and the man was anything but reactionary; if he said it was bad, it was bad. Code Red was never anything less. They weren't on assignment right now, though. Had someone else's op gone sideways?

The four of them packed through the door to the conference room behind their boss. The massive table that dominated the space was empty, but at the end of the room the wide-screen TV hanging on the far wall blared one of the local channels. The sound assaulted Dain's ears as his eyes adjusted to what was on the screen: a close-up of a female reporter he recognized from the usual early morning newscast holding a microphone to her red lips, the wind blowing her blonde hair into her eyes as she spoke.

"Officer Mays, what can you tell us about the situation? Any updates?"

The camera panned to a petite, dark-haired policewoman Dain recognized as one of the Public Information Officers at the Atlanta PD. "No updates as of yet. We are still establishing communications with the suspects and determining how many hostages are currently in the building."

"Is the entire building at risk?"

The glint of impatience in Mays's eyes wasn't reflected in her words. "Not at this time. All floors except the top have been evacuated. Only the fourth floor suite is involved."

"Where—"

Dain had barely gotten the word out of his mouth when the camera panned back behind the anchorwoman to the building in question. A familiar building. The one that held Georgia Financial Management Services.

Livie.

No. Fuck no. "Jack!"

His boss stood on the opposite side of the table, the office phone to his ear, but he jerked it down to tell Dain, "I'm trying to find out. Hang on."

The blonde was speaking again. "For those who are just joining us, would you please recap what is known at this point?"

Officer Mays nodded. "We received a 911 call this morning alerting us to a situation at Georgia Financial. Responding officers determined that gunmen were present, as were employees we believe are being held hostage. Negotiations are forthcoming, and in the meantime, we have asked the public to avoid this area until the situation has been resolved."

"Do we know how many hostages are inside? How many gunmen?"

Mays's face revealed nothing. "Not at this time. We want to assure the public that the APD will do everything possible to resolve this situation. The safety of the hostages and of our citizens is of paramount concern." With a nod at the camera, Mays walked away.

As the anchor promised more information soon and tossed the segment back to her cohort in the studio, Dain fought for breath. "King, I want to know what they know," he barked.

"I'm on it," King said roughly behind him before rushing from the room. Their PR liaison knew everyone who was anyone at the Atlanta Police Department. Dain gave his team member's assurance an absent nod, his gaze still fixed on the television, the screen now showing the local studio and the male news anchor who normally had the blonde sitting next to him. Dain couldn't remember his name and didn't care. He picked up the remote and muted the chatter.

"Elliot," he snapped.

The only female member of his team stepped to his side. Her petite stature forced her to look up at him, one eyebrow quirked in question. Worry clouded her eyes.

"Go to my desk and get my personal cell."

Elliot nodded and ran for the door. Dain tried to force air in and out while he waited. Based on the strain in his heart and lungs, he was pretty sure he didn't succeed worth a damn. The TV screen was showing a segment on grills. Who the hell cared about grills when his wife could be in danger? But he didn't dare look away in case they showed more news on the standoff.

Jack slammed the phone down on its cradle with a hissed "Fuck." No answers, then. Hopefully King—

Elliot swung through the door. "Here," she said and tossed Dain's cell phone across the room before her short legs could carry her to him. He snagged it out of the air and thumbed it on blindly.

"Come on, come on." Livie had gone in to work early. She would've called—shit! He wasn't thinking straight. Dain, who never lost his cool on a job, couldn't think past the fact that his wife was in that damn building.

"She would've called my office phone if there was a situation, wouldn't she?" Assuming she could call at all, but he refused to think about that. "Can you check my office voice mail?"

"Already done," Elliot said. "No messages."

He blessed her under his breath as his phone came online. A red circle with the number one inside sat in the upper right-hand corner of the phone icon.

One message.

He couldn't breathe.

Forcing himself not to tighten his grip until the phone crumbled to bits in his hand, he tapped the icon, navigating his way to voice mail. Livie's name waited at the top of the message list.

He tapped the Play button, then Speaker. Livie's voice broke through the chaos in the room—or maybe that was just his pounding heart.

"*Dain?*"

He swore, the words blistering his throat with the effort to keep them quiet. He upped the volume, not about to miss a single word, a sound, anything.

The sound of her throat clearing came through, then a stronger, "*Dain, there's something wrong here. Stan's— Stan's dead. There's blood.*"

Livie. His wife…she was with a dead coworker. Dain choked on the emotion welling in his chest; he couldn't stop the reaction no matter how unprofessional it was. He'd been in life-and-death situations before, but never… "Wife," he whispered, straining to hear her next words. Would they be her last?

"I can't find everyone else. I'm going to the kitchen. I'm in the kitchen, okay?"

"That's good."

It took him a moment to register Jack's voice. He stared blindly at his boss. "What?"

"The kitchen. There will be weapons there, right?"

Right. And he'd trained Livie to recognize them.

"I've got to go. I'll call your office after I call the cops, okay? I'm all right. I am…"

Livie hesitated on the recording as Dain met Elliot's horrified gaze. "What's the time?" Elliot asked him. When he shook his head, she nodded toward the phone. "The time on the message—what is it?"

He barely had the presence of mind to hit Pause before checking. "Nine thirty?" But that made no sense. Livie had left by seven. Why would she just be arriving at the office at nine thirty?

What time was it now? The clock on the conference room wall read 10:04. So Livie had called the police. She'd said she was going to, so surely—

Jack's voice broke through Dain's daze. "Play the rest."

He stared down at the screen. Thirty seconds were left on the recording. If he played them, would Livie disappear at the end? Or would waiting mean she waited for him in real life too?

Stupid idea. Trying hard to blanket the chaos in his head with a numbness that was usually second nature on an op, Dain clicked Play.

"Dain? Listen, I need to tell you, just in case. I know I'll be fine, but just in case…" A pause. Tell him what? He bit down on the inside of his cheek until he tasted blood, forcing back a scream. Tell him what? *"Dain,*

I'm pregnant. Do you understand? I'm pregnant, husband. I'm having our baby, so you come get me, damn it. Come get us." He heard a sigh that shook so much it told him exactly how scared she was. *"I love you, Dain."*

When the message stopped, so did his heart. Pregnant?

"Fuck!" No way could he be numb after that. Tears stung his eyes, made the phone screen waver in front of him.

He raised the cell to hurl it across the room. Saint's broad hand stopped him midswing. "I think we might need that, Boss."

Dain cradled the phone to his chest and forced himself to get a grip. Blinked away the tears. Took a deep breath. Livie needed him; he had to focus. "I'm so going to spank her ass when this is over," he choked out.

Elliot muffled a laugh behind closed lips.

King rushed into the room, and Dain forced back the emotions clouding his head once again. "What do we know?" he asked, sliding the phone into his back pocket. His team seemed to recognize the shift into work mode; they gathered around the table and started laying out the facts.

"Jerry gave me the basics," King said as he joined them. "Livie works for Georgia Financial, doesn't she?"

Dain didn't need anything else; he saw the truth in King's expression. "How many combatants?"

"More than one; that's all Jerry knows. They received a phone call from a female that was cut short. Officers responding to the call found the doors locked. When they tried to force entry, the suspects showed themselves—and their weapons. Threats against the employees. The cops backed off."

Following procedure. Dain understood it even as his heart protested.

"SWAT is on site now, setting up. The Crisis Negotiation Team is en route. Unfortunately that puts us in a holding pattern."

"The call from the female, who was it?"

King shook his head. "Jerry didn't have a name. Why?"

Because he needed to know if it had been Livie. Because he needed to know if his wife was alive before he completely lost every bit of the control he was known for.

He needed his wife, damn it. He couldn't breathe without her. Couldn't imagine waking up a single morning without her beside him, safe and sound. He wouldn't—no, *couldn't* accept anything else.

If that meant he had to be the one to make her safe, he would. Or die trying.

Chapter Four

The kitchen was empty. Safe, at least for the moment. Olivia slid inside with a sigh of relief and made a beeline for the utensil drawer next to the sink. A single steak knife rested inside, dull from years of slicing and sawing open packages, maybe the occasional piece of meat, but she'd take what she could get. That and a couple of forks went into her slacks pockets. Closing the drawer, she glanced around for more options.

Come on, Livie, think.

The room had a double row of cabinets along one wall, a long utilitarian table and uncomfortable chairs at the back, and a stove, fridge, and trash can on the side closest to the door. No real hiding places, though the niche where the trash can sat, a tiny space between the refrigerator and the back wall, was just big enough for her to slide into. She moved the trash can out but left the broom. Added a spray canister of Lysol from the cabinet beneath the sink. It was too heavy to carry around with her—did no one actually use the stuff?—but in a pinch she could spray several feet away. What else?

Plastic dishes and old cookie sheets. She slid one metal pan into her hideaway, then tucked her body into the small space and allowed herself to relax back against the wall for a moment. Dain's voice in her head urged her to slow her panicked breathing, her racing thoughts. She couldn't. The weight of her child in her womb, of Stan's dead body, of the unknown—

they wouldn't allow her calm. She had to do something, but what?

Not much, if her little stash was anything to go by. But there was one thing she could do. Her cell phone was warm from her overheated body as she pulled it from her trouser pocket. Olivia congratulated herself on her barely shaking fingers as she woke the phone and quickly dialed 911. It only took three tries to get it right.

"Nine-one-one. What is your emergency?"

Her mind blanked. *Deep breath, Livie.* "I think my coworker was murdered."

A brief pause shot her panic back up. Would they believe her? Think this was a prank? What did she really know, after all, other than that Stan was dead?

"Okay, ma'am, can you give me your name and address?"

Walking the dispatcher through the basics seemed to take forever. The need to beg for them to contact Dain, to get through to her husband choked her, but she pushed it aside. She'd talk to Dain when she finished with the police. If she finished with the police…

"Describe what you saw, please, Olivia."

The image of Stan lying on the blood-soaked carpet was one she'd never forget. "I can't find anyone else; my coworkers, I mean. I heard…"

"Heard what, ma'am?"

"I heard arguing, fighting. In the hall at the front of the office. I didn't go up there." Her baby had to stay safe, which meant Livie had to stay safe. "I don't know what to do."

"You're doing exactly the right thing. You've found a secure location and you've called us. We have officers already dispatched to your location. Now, Olivia—"

Livie! She wanted to scream at the woman to call her Livie, to stop calling her anything, to just shut up so she could have a complete breakdown now that she wasn't alone in this hellish situation. She did none of those things. Dain and her baby were counting on her to be smart, to get out of here alive.

And then the dispatcher's words registered. "…door lock?"

"What?"

"Does the door to your room lock?"

She darted a quick glance around the fridge. "No." The door was one of those without a turning handle, and she didn't see a key hole for a lock.

"Is there another exit? Anywhere you can safely exit the building without going back to the main office?"

Of course! She was being so stupid. Adrenaline was fucking with her brain, as Dain would say. They'd probably need to talk about his language before the baby was born.

"There's a stair access door at the end of this hall," she whispered, the idea of going back out there stealing the strength from her voice. Could she not just crawl into the cabinet under the sink and hide her way through this?

"Can you reach the access door without being seen?"

"Anything's possible," she said, not really being sarcastic. She didn't know where the threat was, so she figured that gave her equal chances of getting out or being caught, right?

What would Dain do?

The thought of her husband gave her the courage she needed as she moved back to the kitchen door, heart thumping in fear. She had to try this. She had to get back to Dain, and she had to keep her baby safe. Staying here wasn't guaranteed to accomplish either goal. So she reached for the handle, her fingers tingling with terror.

"Okay, Olivia, I'm going to stay on the phone with you. I want you to see if you can make it to the door. I'm right here with you," the woman told her, voice calm and compassionate. It helped, right up to the moment she placed her fingers on the air-chilled metal of the door handle.

Now she knew how heroines in horror movies felt. Grasping the bar sent her pulse soaring; twisting it made her light-headed. But no bogeyman jumped out with a butcher knife when she eased the door open. The hallway was silent as she slipped out.

"Olivia?"

Fear constricted her lungs, cutting off the air she needed so desperately, but she managed to squeeze out, "Hallway's clear."

The woman murmured an agreement but stayed silent otherwise, seeming to sense the tension of the moment. Olivia eased the kitchen door almost closed, then scooted down the hall in the opposite direction from the office.

There were two emergency-exit staircases, one in the lobby beyond the elevators, and one at the end of this hall. She tried to make herself walk normally to the door instead of creeping like she was, in reality, one of those bubbleheaded horror-movie heroines, but she couldn't help bending over slightly, if only to try to see the stairway door sooner. Every step seemed to take forever. Every breath strained in her lungs. Every second—

The door came into view. Olivia's breath rushed out in relief, her steps speeding up to a trot as she rushed forward.

The metal of the push bar seemed ice-cold against her panic-heated skin. She savored the feel as she pressed as quietly as she could to open the door. The bar slid inward, but…

Nothing.

Had they locked the staircase door? Was it even lockable? Surely that would take someone from maintenance. No one in their office that she knew of had a key to the staircase doors.

"It won't open!"

"Olivia—"

The dispatcher's words were submerged beneath Olivia's panic. Again and again she tried to open the door, each time with the same result. A whimper escaped. "No no no no no!"

A loud whistle in her ear woke her up to the fact that she was making far too much noise. She jerked her hand off the useless bar.

"It's all right, Olivia. Listen to me. Go back—"

A muffled curse at the opposite end of the hall snapped her attention away from the phone.

Shit. Get yourself together, Livie!

It was Dain's voice in her head. Dain, who would be disappointed if she let him down by getting herself captured. Dain, who would be devastated, left alone if anything happened to her.

She was already moving as she whispered, "Someone's coming."

"Get in the kitchen, Olivia. Do it now."

She didn't have the air to tell the woman she was obeying. The fifteen steps between the stair door and the kitchen stretched like a chasm she would never be able to cross in time, but she did. She crossed it, opened and closed the door gently, noiselessly, with extra care, then slid into the tiny space beside the fridge. Only then did a full breath fill her lungs. "I'm okay. I'm okay."

"That's good. You're okay. Stay on the line with me."

The whoosh of air pressure as the door opened echoed through the still room. Olivia went rigid. The dispatcher spoke reassurances in her ear, the sound a distraction she couldn't afford right now. Without responding, she pulled the cell away and clicked End. Slid the phone into her pocket. Exchanged it for the first utensil that came to hand: a fork.

The door hinges creaked lightly.

Oh God. Dain!

Olivia closed her eyes, refusing even to breathe as the moments stretched out like taffy. Memories of her childhood filled her head, playing hide-and-seek with her sister and brother in their old house, squatting in the back of the dark closet with her eyes shut—because if she couldn't see someone, they couldn't see her, right? But squeezing her eyelids together couldn't keep out the sound of that first cautious footstep crossing the linoleum floor.

Her fist tightened on the fork until the edges dug painfully into her palm as she waited. Prayed.

Could she crawl into the space behind the fridge? Her brain said no, but her body shifted instinctively, seeking refuge in the too-small crack at her side. Her foot bumped the canister of Lysol, knocking it over, sending a loud clatter through the room.

Heavy steps rushed for her position, and then everything slowed to a crawl.

Olivia bent down. The scrambling fingers of her empty hand found and gripped a cool metal cylinder.

A shadow stretched along the floor in front of her. Big, so big. She raised the Lysol high.

A tall, heavy man, swarthy, with a ragged beard and mustache covering the broad lines of his lower face, rounded the refrigerator. His black eyes held a mean light as they fell on her hiding place. He wore nice clothes—business casual, she thought a bit hysterically—but they couldn't disguise his depravity; it was in his scent, in the faint whiff of body odor that filled her nose, the sharp smell of testosterone and lust that rose from the crisp button-down shirt and pants.

She knew everyone here, even the janitors. Even the tenants in the suites in the lower three floors. This man was a stranger—and a dangerous one, dress clothes or not.

Recognition, then satisfaction flashed across the man's face, and when he laughed, Olivia shivered.

"Damn, look what I found." His tongue stroked across his half-hidden lips, leaving behind a slick gleam. "Who are you?"

He wanted to carry on a freaking conversation? "Get away from me!"

He ignored her demand, his hard eyes running over her like a dirty washrag, lips smirking. "Sure." Then he lunged.

Olivia didn't wait. The blast of disinfectant hit the man point-blank in the face. He reared back, fingers digging into his eye sockets as his howling filled the room.

Too loud, too loud, too loud!

One big paw of a hand reached for her. Instinct brought her arm up to block him, slapping his hand away. She couldn't let him touch her, couldn't stand his fingers on her skin, her body.

The man roared his anger, spittle flying. "Come'ere, bitch!"

Her lungs seized up, but her body didn't need air; it worked on instinct without it, without time to think. She saw the threat in his eyes, the determination to hurt her as much as possible. In a split second her back hand came up, fork clenched hard inside her fingers.

She bit back a sob. Far too slow and yet so, so fast, the fork arced through the thick air, a blade slogging through mud with deadly intent. Light flashed off the tines as it went from the shadow of the fridge to the glare of the room, and then it sank deep into the man's neck, right below the ragged edge of his beard.

Right into his jugular. *Thank you, target practice.*

She tried to ignore the rubbery feel of resistance as she forced the fork as far into his neck as she could. Blood popped out like she'd speared a juicy piece of fruit, splattering her face. A quick jerk back and she sank the fork in a second time, earning a pained grunt from the man, as if his body only now registered the ripping and tearing of flesh. His hands released their hold, his muscles going limp and heavy.

He landed directly on her. Olivia's head slapped the wall behind her as he shoved her backward, the lapels of his sport coat opening to enfold her, cage her, smother her. His body pinned hers. She closed her eyes and tried not to gag—until the hard pooch of his belly made contact with hers; the obscene intimacy was more than she could endure. A hard push sent him toppling to the floor like a rag doll.

She stood there against the wall, panting and fighting the urge to throw up, for a long time. When she could force herself to look down, she saw him sprawled on the floor, fork sticking from the side of his throat, blood spreading in a dark red stain below his head. Those mean eyes stared at the ceiling, wide and blanked of everything but shock. She looked, tried to process what was before her, the fact that she'd killed this man, taken his life, but it seemed unreal. Impossible. It couldn't have—

A faint choke came from his still form. His throat worked, the barest of movements, like he was trying to swallow. And then a moan of air escaped his lungs. The last breath he would ever release.

Olivia threw up on his legs.

Chapter Five

"We assure you, Mr. Quinn, that the situation is under control. Law enforcement has established containment of the incident site and control of the vicinity via measures dictated by the situation. As you know, we must assure the safety of the general public—"

"Don't quote me the manual, Hedlon," Jack growled at the phone in his hand, currently set to speaker. "I already know it. 'The team leader will have the authority and responsibility to use *any available resources* to negotiate successfully, as long as the area remains secure, personnel are not placed in danger, and the safety of hostages is not compromised.'"

Dain loved it when Jack quoted their own policies-and-procedures manual back to them. Hedlon, not so much.

"Your team would guarantee violating all three of those provisions."

"You have the possibility of one less hostage if you do what I've asked."

"You don't know that."

"Yes, I do!"

There was nothing wrong with his boss's lungs; his angry words pinged the van walls like a rain of bullets. Dain's lungs hadn't worked right since the moment he'd walked into that conference room this morning. And the knowledge that Livie hadn't called back like she'd said she would was a heavier weight than the Kevlar vest King was currently strapping him into.

"I will not send a civilian into a hostile situation."

"Then send in your own men," Jack countered.

Dain bit back his protest. Much as he wanted to storm the fucking building and get his wife out of there, the truth was that anyone getting to Livie would make her safe. Unless the person getting to her was one of the gunmen. He refused to think about that; he couldn't, not and do what needed to be done.

"Jack really should just stop," Dain murmured, more to himself than King, though his teammate answered anyway.

"You know Jack." With a final slap on Dain's chest, King turned in the tight confines of the vehicle to grab a fully loaded equipment belt. "Never misses a chance to chew asses. And Hedlon is the biggest ass of all."

King's liaison at the APD had given him the basics, but when SWAT arrived at the site, the team on duty had been under the authority of SWAT Commander Hedlon. And Hedlon was as by-the-book as they came. He quoted the book, in fact, as often as he could, just to be sure those around him knew it. JCL teams had endured more than one run-in with the man, but today... Today the commander could go fuck himself. Someone was going in there, and if Hedlon wouldn't send a SWAT officer, well, Dain had a full team ready and willing to back him the hell up.

"I do not answer to you, Mr. Quinn," Hedlon said through the speaker, "but since one of the hostages is close to you, I will tell you this: I will send someone in only when it becomes absolutely necessary. We have a trained Crisis Intervention Team for a reason. If the crisis negotiator cannot make headway, then we will seek alternatives. In the meantime, I will not risk setting the suspects off. Is that clear?"

Saint turned from his seat at the comm station, his middle finger raised and pointed directly at the phone. Elliot snorted.

Jack ignored the byplay. "How long before the negotiator makes contact again?"

For reasons known only to Hedlon, he actually answered instead of shutting Jack down. "Fifteen minutes."

I'm not waiting that long.

Dain shook his head at Jack, a quick jerk to indicate the "negotiations" were over. Hedlon wouldn't give in, but neither would they. As he reached for the sliding door to the van, Jack gave him a grim nod in return. "I'll go over your head if I have to, Hedlon," he said.

Dain didn't bother listening to the rest. Jack would keep the man tied up, completely unaware they'd subverted his commands until after the fact. They'd deal with the fallout when Livie was safe.

Elliot and Saint followed him onto the street. Each was vested and loaded up in the exact same uniforms the patrol officers on the perimeter of the scene wore. Of course, they didn't bear the word *SWAT*, and they had a few things hidden up their sleeves—and other places—that the regular cops didn't. Thank God for Saint. The man kept their tech as cutting edge as he did their weapons. Equipment was Saint's baby.

Baby.

Dain's head spun. "Are we ready yet?" he asked hoarsely, turning back to face his team. His gaze fixed on the flash of light off the crucifix around Saint's neck where he monitored radio chatter at the comm. He knew his teammate had already said a prayer for Livie; it was his way. Dain whispered a hasty, unfocused companion to it under his breath, then closed the van door.

Elliot and King followed as he jogged across the street.

The area was quiet, partly due to the police blockade a few blocks over and partly due to the bulletins on radio and TV asking citizens to avoid the area. Dain took full advantage, using empty lots and back alleys to travel the half a mile to Georgia Financial's building on the corner of Eighty-third Street. Next door stood a city parking garage. Dain, Elliot, and King approached from the south, jogging quickly along the concrete walls of the parking structure until the back end of Livie's office building came into view. Dain dropped behind a dumpster and squelched his radio to let Saint know they were in place.

A single *click* confirmed his message had been received.

The grounds weren't extensive. The back of the building held a small parking area for deliveries and a park-like strip of trees and bushes and grass, about fifteen feet wide, along three sides of the lot. Nothing else. The door Dain needed to reach waited smack in the middle of the back wall—and two of Atlanta's finest stood, alert and guarded, right in front of it. Thank fuck one of them happened to be Officer Ford, King's insider. The uniform with him was an unknown, but Dain would take him out—gently—if necessary. One way or another, he was going through that door.

He'd learned patience in the military, but nothing was harder than waiting there, knowing he was so close to Livie but unable to get to her. Saint needed confirmation first. When Officer Ford brought a finger up to his earpiece and nodded, Dain figured Saint had gotten it. A double *click-click* sounded through his own earpiece, making his supposition fact.

His muscles tensed to move out.

"Dain…"

Elliot's hand was on his sleeve, urging him to look at her. The woman had been clawing at the walls wanting to go in with him, but he'd refused. She and King would accompany him only as far as the door; he had a better chance of remaining unnoticed if he was alone inside. "We've been through this, little Otter."

Their not so fun-loving teammate growled up at him, the sound even more intimidating given its tiny source. Dain resisted the urge to lay his hand on her head. Elliot hated any sign of affection on the job, not that she tolerated much off the job. The only thing she hated more was any implication that she was tiny. Patting her head met both criteria, and he'd like to keep his hand for the trip inside, so he didn't risk her biting it off. He couldn't keep his look from conveying a mix of gratitude and indulgence, though.

"I know exactly where she is, remember?" he reminded her quietly. "I'm going straight there, straight back. In and out. This isn't about a confrontation, I promise." Not that he had a problem with confrontation, but only when the situation required it. Livie's didn't, not yet.

"Damn right. You get your woman out; that's all," King muttered from his position behind Otter.

"I will." *You come get me, husband.*

As he stood up, he held the image of Livie in his mind, sitting in her favorite armchair near the fireplace in their home, a newborn babe cuddled in her arms. The image of their future. Dain wouldn't leave that future to anyone else.

He gave his team a final once-over. "Let's do this shit."

They moved out.

The second uniform had his gun drawn before the team was halfway across the lot. Good eyes. Dain ignored the threat and kept going. Ford talked low and fast in the meantime.

"Boss?"

He shook his head at Elliot. Either Ford would get through to his partner or Dain would.

"What would you do if your wife was in there?" Ford demanded as they reached the sidewalk surrounding the building.

"You can't decide what's best here! We follow orders; you know that." But the officer had holstered his gun. Dain took that as a positive sign.

"I'm not here to interfere with your op," he assured the man. His muscles quivered with the need to barrel through the blockade and into the building, but he kept it in check—barely. An alert before he had Livie out could blow everything to hell.

The officer shook his head stubbornly. "Like hell you aren't."

Dain glanced down to the name tag on prominent display on the man's uniform. "Wakeland"—he pointed up at the windows lining the building above them—"see that window up there? Fourth floor, first on the left. That's where my wife is. I know because she called me. She's there, and she's waiting for me to come get her before those bastards at the front of the building take her hostage too." He paused, letting that sink in. "I can get her and get out; you know that. Your boss thinks his protocol will save lives; I really hope he's right. But my wife won't become a hostage if I can do anything about, Hedlon be damned." He stepped closer. "Do you want to risk that? Risk them finding her before I can? Do you want one more hostage on your conscience, or do you want her out of the building and safe before those bastards even know she's there?"

Every nerve in his body did a jig as he watched the officer's mouth tighten, refusal and agreement warring in his expression.

"You know he's right, Wakeland," Ford said. "No one has to know."

The uniforms exchanged a long look. "Only him?" the partner asked. "Not the other two?"

Despite Elliot's protests, that had been the agreement. One man in, one man and one woman out.

"Just him," Ford agreed.

A sharp nod. "Fine. You should know, they've locked the door up there."

Dain patted his pocket. "No problem. I'll take care of it." He turned to look at his team.

"We'll wait here, Boss," King assured him, tapping his earpiece to remind Dain they'd be listening in if he needed their help.

Elliot didn't repeat her protest, though he could see her biting her tongue on it. Dain grinned down at her. "Be thinking up baby names, Otter," he told her.

"I guess Asshat is out, huh?"

"I'll ask Livie." He turned toward the door.

"You sure as hell better, Dain," she warned him right before he slipped inside.

Chapter Six

Cool dark enclosed him as the door slid shut at his back. Dain waited a moment for his eyes to adjust, for the concrete staircase leading upward to differentiate itself from the surrounding walls in the faint glow of the EXIT light above his head, making certain no one waited nearby. Only then did he start up the stairs.

The quiet always took on an eerie quality on an op. It was the same quiet that normally encased a dark night or an unused part of a building or an empty room, but the urgency, the risk changed the air he breathed, the lack of sound taking on weight in his ears. He breathed in and out in rhythm with his silent steps, wrapped himself in control as he rounded each bend of the cool metal railing. In less than a minute, he was at the door with a large black four on the adjoining sign.

No window, no way to peek. And when he turned the handle, the door didn't budge. Locked, just like the officers said. That meant whoever was doing this knew the back area of the offices, had been there at some point to secure it. Had they found Livie already?

He pulled a set of picks from his equipment belt and went to work.

He hadn't been to the back rooms more than once. From the position of the staircase he knew he'd be at the end of the hall, and that the kitchen waited only a few feet away. Picturing the layout in his mind, he fiddled with the pick until he heard and felt the lock give. His hand dropped automatically to the GLOCK at his hip, drawing the weapon smoothly as he pocketed his tools. A quiet pull on the door and he was in.

The hallway was empty, all doors shut. He took a moment to settle the exit door back into its jamb without a sound, then glided on silent feet toward the kitchen.

Deep breath. He stopped outside the room and listened, but if Livie was in there, he couldn't detect it. No sound. He released the air from his lungs at the same time he gave the door a push.

She stood with her back to him. He knew it was her immediately, the long line of her back and fiery red hair as familiar as his own reflection. A glance down the hall confirmed they were alone for now.

He moved inside.

The click of the latch closing caught Livie's attention.

Next thing he knew, there was a fork coming at his face. Livie's expression shone like a Valkyrie, fierce and bright, a mama bear protecting herself and her cub. No recognition, nothing but the determination to fight to the death—with a fork. Christ.

Dain caught her hand easily, gently, pulling her close with his grip on her wrist. "Livie, it's me. It's Dain."

Her eyes seemed to clear, focusing on his face. He knew the moment she recognized him through the adrenaline coursing in her veins. That fierce expression crumpled, and so did his wife, right to her knees.

"Livie, baby." Dain kept his voice low, but he couldn't keep the emotion out of it, the relief. Dangerous on an op, but this was no ordinary op. He dropped to his knees next to his wife and pulled her trembling body into his arms.

Resting the GLOCK on the floor next to him within easy reach, he listened to the soft sound of her crying, felt her shake, let the knowledge that she breathed sink into his soul even as he ran careful hands over her, searching for wounds, for anything wrong, and maybe just reassuring himself that she was real, not a figment of his needy imagination. His touch on her body was as familiar as breathing, grounding him in the moment.

The soldier part of him, ever present, scanned the room for threats. That's when he saw what lay on the floor beyond her. Or who. A hoarse "fuck" left his lips.

She'd put at least one fork to good use. Knowing what must've pushed her to that point, he felt nothing but satisfaction at the sight of the body. The faint scents of blood and vomit and disinfectant registered in his nose as he hugged Livie closer, breasts pressed hard to chest, letting her absorb his strength like he absorbed her tears. Her name escaped, a rough whisper he repeated over and over, a litany drawing her back from the darkness.

Time slowed, wrapping them in a muffled sense of safety until Livie's crying finally shuddered to a stop. Dain eased back, but when he tried to kiss her, she jerked away.

"No. No, wait. I have to—" She broke off, stumbling to her feet, lunging for the sink before she fully stood. When she turned the water on full blast, he wondered distractedly if she thought he'd be offended that she hadn't brushed after throwing up. He couldn't care less. He wanted his wife in his arms, her mouth against his, the assurance that she was alive and well undeniable to more than his eyes.

Her ragged whispers shredded his suppositions and protests into confetti. "Wash him off. Wash him off. Wash him…"

Dain's gut twisted hard.

Walking slowly up behind her, he settled first one hand, then the other loosely onto her hips. Livie didn't startle, didn't break her focus on the water rushing into the sink, into her cupped fingers. He tightened his grip, determined to wait until she was ready but unable to deny himself the feel of her, solid, real, beneath his hands, against his body. He couldn't ignore the juxtaposition of this moment and this morning, how different the circumstances despite the fact that he'd held her just like this in the shower a few hours ago. Careful not to scare her, he curved his body around hers, sliding his arms beneath her belly to hug her close, needing to comfort her almost as much as she needed to wash.

When she finally turned the water off, Dain fished around in the drawers until he found a hand towel to dry her with. He held her still as he swiped the water from her face. "Livie, tell me what happened."

"He heard me." She sucked in a rough breath, but her gaze never wavered from his. "I was too loud trying to get the stair door open, and he heard me. I'm sorry."

He shook his head, a fierce heat filling him. "You don't have anything to be sorry for. Not one damn thing, you got that?" He waited for Livie's nod before dropping his gaze to her body. "Did he hurt you?" Blood spattered her clothes, but he didn't see any rips or tears. He tried to breathe away the anxiety of knowing what else might've happened without the aid of a single piece of cutlery. Her silence didn't help.

"Did he, Livie? Talk to me."

She blinked rapidly. "He didn't… I couldn't let him close; I couldn't risk… I couldn't." Her gaze skittered around the room, over the body, then returned to him as if he was her anchor. "I had to protect our baby."

Our baby.

He'd waited as long as he could. Cupping her face, he brought her lips up to meet his descent. Their mouths fit together perfectly, just as their souls did, their bond locking into place as surely as their kiss. Livie's mouth felt cool from the water, but he shared his heat as he forged inside. *I love you.* Maybe another man would feel bad about what she'd had to do, about the man's death, but not Dain—he was a warrior through and through, and so was his wife. He'd rather a hundred evil bastards die than for her to be taken from him.

Don't ever leave me, wife. But he couldn't say it, not right now, not with emotion choking him. Right now he had to get her to safety.

Pulling away reluctantly, he traced a finger across her bottom lip. "A baby, huh? You sure know how to surprise a guy."

Livie's eyes brightened the tiniest bit. "After ten years I have to keep things interesting somehow."

The emotion grabbed hold of his throat and wouldn't let go. "You do that just by breathing, wife."

She leaned her forehead against his, and he heard the faint hitch of her breath in her throat. "I knew you would come for us."

"You're fucking right I would." And speaking of which… "We need to go."

Livie's gaze skimmed the rest of the kitchen without settling on any one thing. "What should we do about…?"

"Leave him. Someone else can take out the trash later."

She didn't argue, just gripped his hand as he turned for the door. Nothing felt more right than that touch, than her trust. It hit him square in the chest every damn time—and every damn time, he thanked God for the gift.

"Ready?" he asked, hand settling on the door handle. A glance back at Livie showed a worried look in her eyes, but she was nodding despite it. "Let's go then. Quietly, okay?"

Another nod.

Dain pulled. The door swung open. He managed a single step into the hallway before the cool circle of a gun barrel landed on his temple.

Chapter Seven

Dain fought when the men tried to separate them. He only stilled when Godzilla, her personal captor, pulled a knife to lay against her neck. Olivia cringed away from the cool edge stroking her skin, but holding Dain's rage-filled eyes helped her keep her shit together. Dain needed to focus, and not on a possible threat to her. He could overcome anything, she firmly believed that, except them hurting her. The precious bond between them anchored her and, she hoped, anchored him while the head of their merry band of hoodlums patted Dain down.

If you could call it that. The leader's version of a patdown made the TSA look like a bunch of drunk frat boys. Dain growled more than once as he was divested of Kevlar vest, weapons; even his boots and earpiece were yanked off his body. She couldn't see the zip tie they'd used to secure his wrists behind his back, but from the way the skin around his eyes tensed, it was much tighter than it needed to be.

Helplessness tugged at her. If she was beside him, the dull knife still in her pocket might have some use, but she wasn't. Godzilla had kept her a good distance away until Dain was secure; then he'd marched her along the hall, blade still at her throat. She could hear the others following, Dain's grunt as they forced him along, but she couldn't see him, couldn't help him.

At least Godzilla wasn't as smart as his leader. He hadn't secured her hands, nor had he searched her, so the fork and knife she'd hidden in her pockets were still there, waiting for a chance, just like she was. Typical sexist bull would come back to bite them on the ass. At least she hoped so. They had completely discounted her in favor of the obvious danger: Dain.

Their little group rounded the bend near Rosie's desk and proceeded up the front hall toward Cecil's office. No sign of Cecil, though. When Godzilla forced her to a halt outside their largest conference room, the executive one Cecil used for company meetings, she prayed she was about to find the rest of her coworkers behind the door, alive and well. Her heart couldn't take another Stan.

Godzilla opened the door, then shoved Olivia inside. Relief had her sagging in his grip.

Rosie. René. Carla. Even John David. A quick head count came up with nineteen—every employee except Stan and Cecil. All safe. All bound just like Dain and seated against the walls of the conference room. Olivia had no more than a moment to take in all their faces before Godzilla pulled her away from the door with a rough grip on her arm.

The man she'd heard shouting earlier entered, pushing Dain ahead of him. He was slim and neat in his business suit, dwarfed by Dain's size but with enough take-no-shit attitude that she knew he would be no easy target. When he forced Dain to his knees, she had to fight to hold herself back, hold her anger in. Dain might be tough, but she hated seeing him hurt. The primal instinct to protect her mate raged inside her, hard to resist.

The leader leaned casually against the glass of the conference room, focus all on Dain, any concern or fear he might feel hidden completely. Long minutes stretched out under his stare, his silence, finally broken with a single question: "Where did you come from?"

"I came from downstairs," Dain answered. He didn't take his gaze off Godzilla and his knife, ignoring the leader in every way except his words.

The man's mouth tightened, whether at Dain's response or the refusal to acknowledge him, Olivia wasn't sure. She was sure nothing good would come of it when he stepped forward. He was a lefty, his gun in that hand, but the other swung hard. Dain took the slap without so much as a flinch.

Olivia bit down on her lip, tasting blood, but her cry of protest stayed inside. The other hostages weren't as successful—more than one muffled shout echoed around the room.

"Don't lie to me," the man snapped, voice as sharp as the crack of his hand had been. "The cops have this place surrounded; we know that. They wouldn't allow a civilian to cross their line."

True. How had Dain managed to get inside?

"He's a cop, yeah?" the third man asked, eyeing Dain's uniform while stroking his semi-auto like it was a lover. Livie hid her disgust behind what she hoped was a blank stare.

Dain kept his silence.

The first man's gaze trailed from Dain to Olivia. "Not a cop," he said decisively. "I just got off the phone with the negotiator. They wouldn't risk the hostages by going around me. No"—he tapped a finger against his chin—"I'm not sure how he managed it, but he's not a cop. He's here for her."

And just like that, the man had disarmed Dain of more than his weapons. All he needed to control his strongest hostage was to figure out his motives, and he'd done that easily. Dain didn't need weapons or even the use of his hands to kill someone, but he wouldn't make a move with two guns and a knife aimed her way. He was holding back because of her, and this man knew it, knew he held all the power.

Or thought he did. One look into Dain's eyes told Olivia a far different story. With Dain in this room, their baby stood a much higher chance of surviving. So did the rest of them.

At least the cops were negotiating. The relief she felt at the knowledge was echoed in the eyes of Olivia's coworkers as she glanced toward them. Rosie, chin only a little bit wobbly, gave her the slightest dip of her head. They were okay; Olivia just had to help her husband keep them that way.

The leader moved toward her. "The important question here is, who are you?"

"Who are you?" she countered, feeling the nudge of steel against her Adam's apple.

"Me?" A dark brow shot up. "You don't know me?" Once more he eyed her up and down. "No, you're not the kind of woman who would know me. Him, now?" He nodded at Dain without looking away. "He'd know me, I bet. Nat Kelly."

Olivia drew a blank, just like he'd said she would. Dain's face revealed nothing, though his gaze had locked on the man like a cobra's.

Well, that gave her nothing to work with. "So…why are you here? Why did you k-kill Stan?" she asked, stumbling over the words. Disbelief still filled her despite the fact that her friend and coworker's body lay not far outside the door, in a pool of dark, drying blood. Why would anyone kill him, much less a stranger?

"Was that his name?" Kelly turned his head to glance down the hall, shrugged his shoulder. "He refused to give me what I want."

"And what is that?" Dain asked. After years of reading him, knowing him intimately, she could tell he at least had a clue.

"Money."

A bark of laughter escaped without Olivia's permission. "You came here for money?"

Kelly's smile peeked out from beneath a dark mustache, giving him a boyish look that wreaked havoc with Olivia's perceptions. "Of course."

That was ridiculous, but Kelly didn't seem to sense the irony—or didn't let on that he did. She drilled the man with her stare, demanding he explain.

Her demand seemed to amuse him. "She's a hellcat, isn't she?" he asked Dain. The muscle in Dain's cheek flexed, but he didn't answer.

Kelly shrugged. "If you've got a problem with us being here, talk to your boss. It's all on him."

"Stan?"

"No. Your boss. Cecil Derrick."

Of course. He'd been arguing with Cecil when she first arrived. She glanced over her coworkers, the conversation she'd heard making more sense now that she was in the room with them. What didn't make more sense was how Cecil was involved with Kelly. Their CEO was nice, unassuming—a family man, not a criminal. She doubted he knew anyone who owned a gun, much less men like this.

"See, Mr. Boss Man Derrick owes some very important people a large sum of money. Money he hasn't paid back in a timely manner. That's where we come in." He jerked up his gun, his implication obvious. Olivia's heart gave a hard thump. "We're here to collect."

"Collect money?"

One dark eyebrow went up at her question. "What else?"

"That would be a fine plan if we actually had money here, but we don't," Olivia pointed out. "Not even petty cash. We don't need it. Nowadays no company does unless they're retail; everything is online." That was Modern Business 101.

"We know." Kelly stepped closer, that gun aimed right at her belly. Instinctively Olivia sucked in her stomach, as if the hardened muscles could protect the baby from a bullet. "But access codes have to be on hand for companies to access funds online. I believe…Stan? Was that his name? I believe Stan had the access codes we wanted. Unfortunately for him"—he glanced toward the hall again—"he did not want to provide them for us. He objected. Forcefully."

A chill skittered across her skin. "So you killed him?"

How could a man so immoral have eyes seemingly clear of guilt? "It's not personal," he said, "just business."

And where was Cecil? If, as Kelly said, he was responsible for all of this, where had he been when Stan was shot? Where was he now?

"You screwed yourself; you know that, right?"

Kelly's eyes slitted at Dain's taunt. He glanced at his crony and jerked his head. The man headed for Dain.

Olivia moved too, no more than a step, but she couldn't ignore the instinct to protect Dain. Her hand slid into her pocket. Godzilla's rough paw stopped her before she could withdraw it.

"What is that?" he growled, his grip tightening on her throat as he pillaged her pocket. Olivia closed her eyes and pressed herself into his body with all the force she could manage. The feel and smell of him made her want to gag, but she'd tolerate it for even a single millimeter of space between her throat and that damn knife.

The harsh crunch of a fist landing on bone jerked her eyelids open again. A large red bruise marred Dain's cheek.

"Stop!"

"Livie, be still!" Dain's eyes met hers. A slight shake of his dark head warned her to wait. She didn't want to; she wanted to make them hurt like her husband hurt. She wanted them to feel the fear that consumed her every time a weapon swung her way. She wanted—

Kelly stepped between her and Dain, his grin wide. That look scared her more than his anger, though she wasn't sure why. "I never would've thought you had it in you, lady."

"Had what in me?"

His hand came up, making her flinch. Her dull knife and fork looked silly in his heavy fist.

Kelly tsked. "Maybe it wasn't the big guy over there that we needed to worry about all this time." Still grinning, he leaned forward. "Was it you that took out Morris?"

Hot breath washed over her face. All of Kelly's attention was on her; everyone's attention was on her. Would admitting what she'd done keep their focus—and free Dain to make a move?

"Yes."

"Thank you."

She blinked.

Kelly cocked his head, grin still firmly in place. "You saved me from having to do it. Stupid bastard got trigger-happy."

He'd been the one to kill Stan? A tiny kernel of satisfaction settled in her churning belly.

The door to the conference room clicked open, startling her. Kelly's gaze swung in that direction.

Cecil stood in the door. Olivia wanted to be angry with him; if Kelly was telling the truth, it was Cecil who had precipitated all of this. But right now, looking into his ravaged face, she couldn't keep sympathy from rising. The man had aged fifty years overnight, it seemed—his eyes were sunken, grief stark in their depths, his movement stiff with fear. When he caught sight of her in Godzilla's grip, his face sheeted white, and for a moment she thought he might pass out.

"Olivia."

His voice broke, the weight of his despair palpable. Her doubts about his guilt died with a single word. Her name.

Kelly strode toward Cecil, who cringed back into the hall, holding a phone up with a shaking hand.

"The negotiator," he said.

Kelly took the handset with a jerk of his head toward the conference room. "Harris, Jones, lock it down," he barked.

Godzilla released her. He and his cohort changed places with Cecil, slamming the door behind them. Olivia heard the click of a lock, then receding footsteps as their captors walked away.

Cecil turned to her, reluctance in every line of his body.

"God, Cecil." Her throat closed up. When Cecil's tired eyes met hers, the sheen of tears obvious, words deserted her.

Dain didn't have the same problem. "What the hell have you done, Derrick?"

Chapter Eight

Dain pushed himself to his feet. Cecil Derrick, smart guy that he was, jerked back. Not that Dain planned to hit him—he needed the guy to figure out what the hell was going on here, no matter how satisfying a punch might've been.

"Dain!" Livie didn't wait for Cecil's answer. She rushed to his side, her warm hands settling on his straining biceps as he worked the zip tie holding him bound. Seconds later, a light pop signaled his release.

"How did you…?"

Dain turned toward the voice—a young man, maybe twenty, propped against the far wall, his hands behind his back like everyone else. Dain held up a tiny blade for the kid to see. "Hidden pockets." Flexing his sore wrists, he walked over to help the kid to his feet. "What's your name?"

"John David."

The kid turned so his back was to Dain. A quick swipe cut through the zip tie digging into his wrists. Dain handed over the blade. "Here, John David. Take care of everyone else, would you?" When the kid nodded, Dain raised his voice just enough to catch everyone's attention. "People, once your wrists are free, I want you to stay seated with your hands behind your back, okay? No need to clue these guys in that we've got an advantage."

Nods made the rounds. Dain left the kid to his task and turned to Livie. Her sigh of relief was echoed in his soul as he drew her to him. "I'm not hearing an answer, Derrick," he growled over his wife's head.

Cecil's glance ping-ponged between him and Livie as if he wanted to come closer but was afraid of Dain. Smart man.

"Olivia."

His wife's head nudged his chin as she lifted it. "It's Sylvie, isn't it?"

"Yes."

The man's breathless relief grated on Dain's already taut nerves. "Explain."

He knew who Sylvie was, of course. He hadn't met Derrick's family, but he'd helped Livie prep for fundraisers, cook food, anything to help Derrick and his wife, Noelle, get through their only child's diagnosis. Some type of rare genetic disorder, if Dain remembered correctly. The little girl had been through two years of testing and treatments and medication, but last Dain had heard, she was doing well.

Livie's boss kept his focus on her, his concentration fierce, as if the intensity alone would convince her. Of what? That he wasn't to blame for this? That whatever deal he had with Kelly hadn't gotten her coworker killed? Or maybe it was just that looking at Dain made him want to wet his pants. Honestly, Dain was okay with that. If he didn't get an answer in the next five seconds, he might even use it to his advantage.

"Sylvie's...she's sick again."

The sound that escaped Livie told Dain exactly how bad the news was.

"We found out a few weeks ago. The doctors say she needs another round of treatments."

Livie straightened away from Dain. His arms ached at her absence. "Will it work?" she asked Derrick.

The man's shrug, the defeat in his expression had Dain's heart softening the slightest bit. Obviously things didn't look good for Derrick's daughter. "It might. But if she doesn't go through the treatments, they…well, they said she's only got a few weeks at most."

Livie's curse echoed the one in Dain's head. His voice was rough as he asked, "How does that lead to Stan's death and a roomful of hostages?"

Derrick's gaze dropped to the floor then, almost as if he couldn't bear the scrutiny. Good. Harsh as it seemed, Dain could work with guilt; amoral assholes like Kelly couldn't be flip because they just didn't care. Derrick cared, very much.

"I didn't mean for this to happen. I promise, I didn't mean to."

"You borrowed the money from one of Kelly's associates, didn't you?" Dain asked.

Derrick nodded. "I've been borrowing from them for a few months now. I had no choice."

"I thought you made arrangements with the hospital to pay—"

At Livie's words, anger twisted the man's haggard face. "Of course I did! I did everything they told me to do, but it wasn't enough. We're still paying thousands to the hospital every month. There's barely enough money left to cover groceries, much less the mortgage. They're foreclosing on the house, Olivia. On Noelle's car. There's just…nothing left. There's no way to keep my daughter alive without money."

66

His words choked off. "My wife will not lose her daughter. I don't care what it takes."

"So you—"

"I found a way to get the money I needed, okay? Nothing wrong with that."

No, there was nothing wrong with that. It was reasonable, normal. Your child was sick, so you found a way to pay for it, just like any good parent would do. Just like Dain would do.

And yet the consequences of that single decision had been anything but reasonable or normal.

Livie met Dain's eyes. He could see the understanding, the sympathy for Derrick's situation warring with the knowledge that her coworker was dead, her own child in danger because of this man's actions. Her gaze pleaded with him to tell her what to do, how to fix this. He wouldn't let her down. He just needed to come up with a plan.

"Why did Kelly come here?" he asked Derrick.

"The first payment was due last week."

"And you didn't have it."

"Sylvie had her first treatment last week. The doctor required a deposit. It took most of what I owed, but they wouldn't let me put off the payment. And then Kelly showed up—"

Because his boss wouldn't take partial payment either. "And Stan?"

A tear escaped Derrick's eyes then. "He tried to run. One of Kelly's thugs—not one of those two," he said with a jerk of his chin toward the door, "but a different one, he shot…"

A sob choked off in Livie's throat, muffled behind her hand. Dain slid his palm down her spine, back up, trying to calm her, to give her strength.

"He's the one in the break room, isn't he?" she asked him.

"I think so." He knew so, but dwelling on it wouldn't get them out of here. He met Derrick's eye, told the man to proceed with a jerk of his chin.

Derrick cleared his throat. "Everyone saw Stan and went nuts. That's when Kelly corralled us all in here. They made me tie everyone up so they couldn't cause problems." He scrubbed his hands over his cheeks, his eyes. "I'm sorry, Olivia. I really am. But you have to understand; without that money, Sylvie won't get her treatments. I needed it."

Dain felt a quiver go through Livie's body where she continued to lean against him. "You think I care about the money?" she asked sharply. Dain knew exactly what she was thinking. Yes, stealing was wrong, but it was money, not a life. He couldn't imagine choosing between his child's life or death. "We would've helped you, Cecil. We would have; you know that."

"It's not enough," he said, each word heavy with sadness. "I never meant for any of this to happen."

Intentions wouldn't bring Stan back to life, though. And they wouldn't protect Livie and their baby if Kelly or his men were pushed too far. The negotiators would do their best, but giving Kelly what he wanted and getting everyone out of here was the only way to guarantee no one got hurt.

With his arm around her back, Dain urged Livie across the room to a quiet corner. "We need a plan, wife."

"I know."

He turned at the wall so he faced the conference room door, then pulled her against him. "Doing okay?"

Her smile was strained. "The baby's not liking all this tension. I'm trying very hard not to throw up."

His baby, his wife. He squeezed his eyes shut for the briefest moment. When he opened them, he caught the attention of an older woman sitting not too far away and nodded toward a table in the corner of the room. "Ma'am, can you bring us one of those bottles of water?"

The woman hurried to retrieve a bottle. "Here you go, Olivia," she said as she handed it over. "You doing okay? They didn't hurt you, did they?"

"I'm good, Rosie. I promise."

Rosie retreated to her space along the wall.

Livie took a tentative sip, held it in her mouth, then swallowed. When that stayed down, she sipped again. Dain waited patiently until her gaze latched on to his once more. "What are we going to do?"

His brain had been puzzling over that question as he took care of Livie. "What do you know about these codes Kelly is looking for?"

"I know he keeps—kept—a copy of them in the safe in his office."

He didn't want to ask, didn't want to put her any more at risk than he had to, but their backs were against a wall here. Livie was the vice president of the department Stan had headed. "Do you know the combination?"

Livie's voice dropped to a whisper. "I think I'm the only one who knows it besides Stan. He was funny about information safety, anything that could tempt an employee, especially with the kinds of sums in those accounts. That's probably why Cecil couldn't access them himself—he doesn't have the combination."

"Okay." He cupped her face, tilting it up until their foreheads met. Her beauty took his breath away, and for a moment he let everything go and just absorbed her, treasured her, assured her with his touch and his look that everything would be okay. And it would; he'd make sure of it. If he couldn't kill the fucker who'd put that fear in her eyes, he'd sure as shit do the next best thing. "They'll be back soon. The negotiator won't keep them on the phone forever. Kelly never intended to be in this situation; he wants out as much as we do. So we're going to give him what he wants: the combination to retrieve those codes."

Livie's breath hitched. "The problem is, even with the codes, he can't leave. The police have this place surrounded, don't they?"

"They do. But Kelly doesn't need to get out; the hostages do. Take away the leverage and he's left holding an empty bag."

"How do we get them out?"

"We don't, wife," he warned her.

"But Dain—"

"But nothing. Your job is to keep you and the baby safe. I'm already having a hard enough time letting you help that bastard. Help me do my job; keep yourself safe, okay?"

"What are you going to do?"

"What I'm good at." He smirked.

Livie laid her cheek against his chest, her breath warm on the tough skin of his neck as she murmured in his ear. "I think that would be difficult in a roomful of people, husband."

"Don't underestimate me," he whispered back. The soft sound of her laugh rang in his ears as he called Cecil over.

When Kelly swept through the conference room door minutes later, Dain and the rest of the hostages had their hands behind their backs, Dain sitting next to the kid who'd freed the others earlier.

"I'm running out of time and patience, Derrick," Kelly announced. "I want those codes, and I want to leave, and you're going to make both happen."

Derrick hesitated.

"Stan wasn't the only one who had those codes, was he? He couldn't be—someone else in the company has to have access, and if it isn't you, who is it? I want to know. Now."

Kelly's demand was deceptively quiet, but still Derrick jumped. He glanced to Dain, then to Livie. Dain noticed his wife's eyes filled with tears. The slight shake of her head gave the perfect touch of resistance.

"No," Derrick finally agreed, "Stan wasn't the only one with the pass codes."

Livie's sharp inhale broke the waiting silence. "No. Cecil, no."

Derrick turned away as if he couldn't bear to look at her. "Olivia knows the codes as well."

Chapter Nine

"Nat Kelly."

King grumbled his opinion of the well-known enforcer under his breath. Elliot agreed with every word, but she kept her gaze blank. No sense clueing in the Bobbsey twins watching them like a hawk. The gunmen had taken Dain's earpiece, but each member of their team had a listening device sewn into the collar of their uniform shirt. One of Saint's little tricks. If the techno-geek had been standing in front of her right this moment, she'd probably do something totally inappropriate. Like hug him.

Good thing he was still back in the van. Her tough-as-nails rep could remain intact.

She gave the younger cop a slight smile as she turned to King. "What now?"

Her lips barely moved, but she knew King was wondering the same thing. And she knew exactly what she wanted to do. Every nerve in her body jittered with the urge to get inside that damn building, to give Dain the backup he desperately needed to rescue Olivia, but she had to think with her skills, not her emotions. Not normally a problem for her. This was Dain, though. The only man she'd ever let close enough to know her secrets, her past. Even if he'd had to get her fall-down fucking drunk for her to spill the truth.

She'd hated him for knowing—for all of two minutes. After that, the relief of not carrying the burden alone took over. Dependence was a weakness;

she knew it, and yet Dain had never made her feel weak. Somehow he'd doubled her strength instead.

She'd do anything for Dain and Olivia. And their baby... God, a baby.

What the fuck had Dain been thinking?

A chuckle escaped. She didn't have to wonder; she knew exactly what the fuck he'd been thinking. Dain left no doubt whatsoever about his feelings for his wife, emotional or physical. It had been an eye-opening experience to get to know a male that open and honorable. And then he'd had to go and make her part of a team of males who kicked ass and treated her like family, and she'd been stuck. She, who'd never allowed herself to put down roots, *ever*, had planted herself in their midst and, wonder of wonders, actually morphed into someone almost...normal.

Yes, she'd do anything for Dain, including take a bullet. She wouldn't even hesitate—not that she ever hesitated when the danger was directed her way. She had very little to lose, after all.

King watched her, his electric-blue eyes hidden behind dark sunglasses. Elliot turned the slightest bit more, putting her back to their uniformed friends.

"King—"

"Don't say it." But he knew without the words; his sigh was filled with resignation. "What do you plan to do, storm the fortress?"

"If I have to."

"Hell no," Saint snapped, the curse crackling through both their earpieces. "We're a team, Otter, not a one-man show."

Saint's use of the word *man* instead of *woman* shouldn't have caused a warm glow in her chest. She ran a hand over her forehead, knocking her baseball cap back before adjusting it lower over her eyes. *I am too fucking close to these people.*

It wasn't a surprise. Nothing crept up on her, including emotions. But the knowledge solidified her determination to get to Dain, no matter what it took.

She spoke softly, sure her teammates could hear her. "Kelly isn't known for overblown violence. He might have ties to Miami and Atlantic City, but not to mass murder." A client here or there, yes, but an entire office building? He had the balls for it, no doubt about that, but something didn't click. "He didn't go into that building looking for a standoff, which means he didn't go in with a shitload of guns and ammo."

"His posse isn't exactly known for their intelligence either," Jack chimed in.

Saint cursed again, this time under his breath. "Don't encourage her, Boss."

"He's not encouraging, just acknowledging what's going to happen," King said.

More than even Dain, King seemed to understand her need to rush in where demons feared to tread, maybe because he shared the trait with her. These were the moments when she looked into his eyes and realized that, like her, all he had left to lose was this team.

Her nod of thanks was shrugged off. Yes, she and King had a lot more in common than he let on.

"They won't be expecting any more company," she pointed out. "And you know I can hide better than either of you." She hated being small, but it did have its advantages. "You just have to manage to get me inside."

"Me?" King rolled his eyes. "Why do I let you drag me into these situations?"

She let her smile answer him. "I owe you."

His gaze lit up with a mercenary gleam. "You're damn right, you do. A couple bottles of Lagavulin 21 ought to do it."

"Ouch." She owed him big, apparently. But when he outlined his plan, she figured he would earn every penny. Maybe even a third bottle depending on how bad they roughed him up.

"What about me?" Jack asked in her ear.

"What about you, Boss?"

"Hey, I'm the one that's gonna keep your asses out of jail…maybe. What do I get?"

"Our undying gratitude." She smirked at King, who winked.

A nod sealed the deal between them. They both turned to face Officers Wakeland and Ford at the same exact moment.

"You have a plan once you're inside?" Saint muttered in her ear as she followed King's silent stalk toward the officers.

"Do I ever?"

Not totally true. She did have a plan: wing it.

King threw her a suspicious glance. Elliot shrugged.

"You better watch her reckless ass, King," Saint muttered.

King lifted his sunglasses just enough to show narrowed blue eyes. "You're lucky we love you, little Otter."

He rushed the door while she was still gaping.

Wakeland took the brunt of King's charge. He'd no sooner brought his hands up and pursed his lips around a warning to stop than King barreled into the officer, who barely managed to stay on his feet. He whipped King around, but her teammate maneuvered so that his hands were just out of reach when Ford made a grab for them. In seconds King had two officers hanging on him like he was a quarterback trying to reach the end zone. Or a civilian trying to enter a crime scene without permission. Luckily his leeches were so busy struggling to subdue him that they didn't notice Elliot until it was too late.

She slipped inside, throwing a smug smile over her shoulder as the door closed. Poor King. If he didn't end up arrested—if they all didn't end up arrested, and that was a big *if* knowing Commander Hedlon—she'd have to add kissing his boo-boos to the scotch he'd requested. And judging from the grappling going on, he'd have plenty.

She made quick work of the stairs. At the top she assessed her six, saw no one following, and entered the fourth-floor door quietly but quickly. The empty hall stretched in front of her, doors closed on both sides. The quiet scuff of her boots on the carpeted floor echoed her easy breathing as she jogged the length of the corridor. At the turn into what she knew from Saint's intel was the main room, she paused.

A glance at the thick black watch dwarfing her wrist showed five minutes had passed since Dain and Olivia and Cecil had hatched their plan. After Cecil's revelation about the pass codes, Kelly had separated the CEO and Olivia from Dain, leaving the team in the dark as to what was happening with Dain's wife. Presumably they would be taking her to get the codes.

Cooperate, Livie. Don't give them a reason to get antsy.

Elliot could hear Dain organizing the other hostages in the conference room. He would take them out through the front doors of the office suite while Livie gave Kelly what he sought. Though Dain couldn't communicate directly to them, he knew they'd be listening. Did he know they were guarding Olivia? Did he know they would protect her with their lives if it became necessary?

He had to know.

A faint murmur of voices came not from her earpiece, but from the main room. Too low for her to make out actual words, but by process of elimination she knew it had to be Olivia's little group. She steeled herself for a quick peek around the corner.

The grisly scene at the head of the hall made her grimace. Raising her focus from the body to the room beyond, she saw Cecil Derrick, the man's striped dress shirt and slacks an odd contrast to the blood blocking the entry to the main room. He was walking toward an office along the back wall, directly in her line of sight. Behind him, Kelly marched Livie across the room at gunpoint. Elliot braced herself to move forward if needed.

Chapter Ten

Their little group walked silently through the empty office. Olivia had to force herself not to bump a wall or scuff a shoe, anything to break the monotony of quiet that filled her ears like a rushing tsunami. Startling one of the three men with guns trained on her would not be good, however. Here in the open of the main room, they seemed especially twitchy. She'd made it this far. A few more minutes—minutes that would allow Dain to free her friends—wouldn't push her to the breaking point.

Cecil led the group through the rows of cubicles straight to Stan's office. Olivia kept her eyes averted from Stan's body, her heart aching. To distract herself as well as the others, she turned to Kelly. "What happens after this, after you have the money?"

Kelly watched her and Cecil with penetrating eyes that seemed to miss nothing. "What happens is I disappear. What happens to Derrick is on him, not me."

Cecil had his hand on the doorknob to Stan's office, but at Kelly's words, he jerked back around. "You aren't going to hand over the money to your boss? What—"

"Of course I will; don't be ridiculous. Not that I'd care if something happened to you, but I have no intention of spending my life on the run from the mob. Cops, no problem. But not the family."

He said the last word with a warmth that made no sense to Olivia, as if the men he was talking about really were tied to him by blood. The thought made her stomach cramp.

Cecil's shoulders slumped, probably in relief. He pushed the door open.

"So you get the money you need, pass it along to your bosses, then what?"

Kelly gestured her ahead of him into the room. "Then I take the little bit extra I skimmed from the accounts and find a nice sunny place to retire."

He'd have to. After this, his face would be all over the news. The only way he could stay in the States and not be recognized was with plastic surgery.

Inside Stan's office Olivia took a slow look around. She'd spent a lot of time in this room with her coworker. Stan had trained her for the past five years to eventually take over the accounting department. Framed photos on his desk showed his frequent fly-fishing trips, the golden retriever he'd adopted last year named, oddly enough, Baby. Where would Baby go now? To Stan's sister? The thought sent Olivia's hand to her belly once more, as if her fingers could shield her child from harm.

Kelly nudged her roughly in the back. "Where is it? Where are the codes?"

"In the safe," she told him with a nod to the corner. Stan's office was the exact opposite of her own: to their right sat his wide oak desk flanked by full bookcases, in the center was a small seating area, but in this office the left-hand corner was taken up with a large cabinet. Olivia walked over to it. Keeping her body between the key-pad lock and the men in the room, she entered a series of numbers, then waited for a beep.

The lock snicked opened.

The heavy door resisted her efforts to open it, but with both hands she managed to pull it away from the safe. As she stepped to the side, Kelly crowded in behind her. Piles of papers lay stacked in neat rows on several shelves. The bottom of the safe contained two square boxes. She reached for the one on the left.

The box was slender, light, barely big enough for the three-ring binder Olivia had seen inside it time and again. She passed it into Kelly's eager hands before turning back to close up the safe.

"What the fuck is this?"

The shout startled her so badly Olivia found herself crouching down, searching frantically for an incoming blow. Instead she saw Kelly, open box in his white-knuckled hands, his body shaking with rage.

The box was empty.

Oh God.

Godzilla charged her. She skittered away, leaving him to rifle through the safe at will. The second box was removed, opened—nothing. Kelly's thug tore the contents apart to no avail. The binder containing the pass codes wasn't in the safe.

"Where is it?" Kelly screamed.

Olivia's heart felt like it would crush her ribs at any moment, it beat so hard. She'd backed herself into the corner opposite the safe, needing the wall at her back, needing to feel safe, and yet what stood out to her in that moment wasn't the guns reappearing or the snarling faces, but the spit that left Kelly's mouth as he screamed. That spit made him look rabid. Terrifying. He stalked her across the room, and every step was in slow motion. Every second, every word, every speck of saliva that left his mouth seemed to travel at the speed of a glacier. She knew he was coming, knew she had to get away, and yet her body remained frozen there in the corner, helpless, paralyzed.

"Boss!"

Godzilla's counterpart stood in the doorway looking out. Between one blink and the next, Kelly turned his head. She knew what he was seeing, knew the moment its meaning registered. His eyes went wide; the vein at his temple popped out. His arm rose, semi-auto pointed straight into the main room.

Dain.

She didn't remember giving the signal to her muscles and bones. She didn't remember crossing the room. All she knew was one moment, her husband's name was choking her, and the next, she rammed into Kelly, arms out, using all her weight to throw him away from the door. But she was too late. She knew it when the *pop pop pop* of gunfire sounded in her ear. When glass shattered at the front of the office suite.

When Kelly swung his arm around, slamming the gun into the side of her head.

Dain heard the shout at the back of the room. One last look showed John David bringing up the rear of the line of Georgia Financial employees hurrying toward the emergency stairs next to the bank of elevators. He was grateful they were out of danger, but they didn't hold his heart. His heart was at the back of the room with his wife. His everything. He wouldn't breathe until she was safe.

And then the glass behind him shattered into a million pieces.

A thousand stinging bees landed on his head and neck. Throwing his arms up to protect himself, he darted away from the raining glass. His desperate eyes landed on Kelly in the doorway of Stan's office, gun up, head turned to look at something behind him. He swung around, and his gun connected with Livie's head.

Dain roared.

Three men charged from Stan's office; three guns pointed directly at him. Dain barely registered the noise of shots fired, but he saw Kelly's henchmen go down. How, why, he didn't care. Every ounce of his will went into his legs, into taking out the man who'd hurt his wife.

The man currently scrambling backward in the face of Dain's rapid advance.

He didn't stand a chance.

Before Kelly could gather enough sense to find and squeeze the trigger of his gun, Dain was there. With a quick roll, he locked the man's hand to his weapon and twisted. The sound of joints popping and ligaments tearing filled him with a primal satisfaction. So did Kelly's scream.

And then the gun was in his hand and Kelly's face was making contact with his knee. Dain let him drop like the garbage he was.

"Dain, no, stop!"

The quiver in Livie's voice amped his rage even higher. His step over Kelly's unconscious body was more of a leap, but that was as far as he got. The sight of Cecil coming through the doorway, his arm strangling Livie's neck, a small handgun pointed at her head, jerked him to a stop.

He'd never felt as helpless as he did in that moment. Kelly and his goons, they at least had practice and control on their side. The likelihood of an accidental shooting was low. But Cecil? The way his hand shook testified to his terror. A single twitch could set the trigger off.

Dain slid a foot forward, then another.

Cecil stumbled to the side, toward the back hall, dragging Livie with him. Her breath caught on a sob.

Dain put his hand up, the free one. The gun hand he slid behind his back—out of sight, out of mind, hopefully. "It's okay, Cecil. It's okay. Don't hurt her."

"Cecil, don't do this. Don't make it worse than it already is."

There was no going back from this, Dain knew. The dozen SWAT members outside assured it. There was no escape for Derrick. Any sympathy the man had garnered faded to nothing when Dain's gaze came to rest on Livie's face. Her eyes were glued to his, her expression stark terror. She knew exactly how precarious her situation was, and it was killing him.

The ragged sound of Cecil's panicked laughter washed over them. The man's eyes shifted back and forth, surveying the room but not really tracking. Derrick had lost it—and he held Dain's world in his arms. "It can't get worse."

"Yes, it can." *I could kill you.* He would, friend or not. He just needed a clear shot.

Using Livie's body to shield himself, Cecil shuffled toward the hallway. "I've got to get out of here, Olivia. Noelle needs me. Sylvie—" His voice broke on his daughter's name. "She needs me. I have no choice. I have to get away before they find us."

"Cecil, don't." Livie's voice shook. "We'll find the money. I'll find the codes, I promise, just put the gun down and let me go."

So the codes hadn't been in the safe as they'd thought. Dain didn't point out that Derrick would never make it to his family without being captured. He simply advanced, heel to toe, heel to toe, getting as close to Livie as he possibly could.

Derrick's finger fumbled at the trigger.

"Don't," Dain growled. "Don't do it."

"Stop, motherfucker!"

The voice came from the hallway behind Cecil and Livie. Small, delicate-looking Elliot inched closer, the warrior side of her on full display. She stalked forward slowly, just like Dain, gun drawn and trained on Cecil, blue eyes filled with cool calculation and a tiny bit of glee as she sized up her prey. That look made suspects sweat, and Cecil was no different. His attention jerked between the threat in front of him and behind, as if he could keep them at bay with a look. The panic in his eyes denied it.

Cecil raised his shaking hand, gun in grip, to point directly at Dain. "Don't come any closer!"

And just like that, Dain could breathe again. Not Livie; her gasp reached his ears, the knowledge that he was far too close to dodge a bullet shining in her eyes. "Put the gun down, Cecil," she begged him. "No one has to die. You don't have to die. You have to live, for Sylvie. Please, please don't do this."

"Everyone freeze. Guns down!"

SWAT was tired of waiting, it seemed. Two officers moved in behind Dain, at least one gun trained on him. The itch at the back of his neck told him so.

Livie squeezed her eyes shut.

"Back off," Dain told the officers over his shoulder. "Just let me get to my wife."

Her eyelids fluttered up, her desperate gaze locked with his. He tried hard to reassure her with a single look that this whole mess would turn out all right. He would make it come out all right.

"Move, sir."

Like hell. "I can't do that."

"Sir, move!" Harder. They were getting impatient.

"I'm ordering you to put your gun down on the floor and get on your knees."

"I can't do that."

"You will comply or—"

"Sir, get on your knees!" A third officer. Dain shook his head, attention on Cecil and the gun in his hand. On Livie.

"Sir—"

"Shut the fuck up!" Cecil roared. The hand holding the gun lowered the slightest bit, reflecting his shift in attention. The white-knuckle grip he had on Livie relaxed.

Dain met Elliot's eyes across the room. Nodded. It was no more than a millisecond, but it was all they needed to plan, to act.

A piercing whistle sliced through the air. Livie jerked her head at the sound, turning toward Elliot.

Elliot dipped her chin, telling Livie what to do.

She dropped—and slid right out of Cecil's distracted hold.

A single shot bit through the air.

It all happened so fast, and yet…not. Dain could hear Livie's knees crack against the hard floor. Saw the buck of Cecil's body as Elliot's bullet found its mark. Livie curling down over her stomach to protect their baby. So fast, and stretching out for an eternity.

For forever. Until Dain reached his wife and pulled her tight into his arms.

Livie. God. She relaxed into his chest, her hands clutching at him, the sound of her breathing blocking out everything in the world but her. Nothing and no one mattered but the woman in his arms. The woman he'd almost lost.

"You're lucky I don't kill that motherfucker myself," he muttered in her ear, rocking gently. "Only reason I don't is because maiming hurts longer, and Elliot already did the damn job for me." Derrick writhed on the floor nearby, howling and clutching his shoulder. Elliot had good aim.

"That's my Dain," Livie said. He could feel the wetness of her tears on his neck, feel the shaking of her body, but her lips curled into a smile against his skin. "We're going to have to talk about your language before the baby comes," she whispered. Goose bumps shimmered cross his neck at the rasp of her lips.

"Talk all you want, wife," he told her hoarsely. "As long as you're in my arms, talk all you want."

Chapter Eleven

Hedlon at least had the good sense to keep his team off Dain as he held his shaky wife. He waited till paramedics arrived to check her over before pissing Dain off.

"Interfering with a police investigation."

"Good thing I did interfere, Hedlon. I got the hostages out; what did you do?" Livie was brushing back a lock of her shining red hair with a hand that shook. Dain wanted to be over there with her, not talking to this prick.

"You circumvented the rules, put yourself and other civilians in danger, put my men in danger—"

Dain snorted at that. "Your men weren't even around. They were downstairs waiting on the negotiators to do their job."

Hedlon took a step toward Dain, the stubborn expression on his face promising trouble. Dain'd had enough. "Don't do it, Hedlon. Just don't." And then, because he knew Jack would expect at least a show of reconciliation, "Look, I understand you're angry. I can even understand how you might think I 'circumvented the rules.'" Dain let his gaze flick over Hedlon's left hand. "You're married. If your pregnant wife was in a situation like this, would you be waiting outside the perimeter for someone to give permission to go get her? Would you?"

Hedlon hesitated. Eyed Dain. Lips tight, he shook his head.

That's what I thought, dickhead.

Hedlon didn't try to stop Dain as he walked toward Livie. He needed his mate in his arms, and he was going to have her. Once he gathered Livie up and turned to sit on the gurney, Livie in his lap, he noticed Hedlon was already gone.

Jack, King, and Saint appeared at the bend of the back hall, directly in Dain's line of sight, and strolled casually toward them. Dain noticed Jack's gaze taking in the chaos surrounding them.

Jack raised his eyebrows. "Well, that was a nice mess."

"Yeah." King was sporting a black eye Dain would ask him about later. Right now it only slightly obscured his glare at Elliot. "Did you have to discharge your weapon? Do you know how much paperwork that involves?"

Elliot squared off with King, hands on her hips—as if that made her appear any bigger. "Considering the compensation, I don't think an hour's paperwork will kill you, big guy. Besides"—she snarled up at him—"you couldn't have done any better."

Considering Elliot had injured all of the assailants but Kelly? No, Dain doubted even he could've done better.

King laid his hand on Elliot's head. "Of course I could, little Otter."

While the rest of them cringed at King's bravery, Elliot punched the man underneath his arm, knocking his hand off her head and rearranging his unguarded ribs if Dain was any judge of force. When Dain joined in the laughter, his body protested with a multitude of aches and pains.

Guess I'm too fucking old for this.

Except he wasn't, was he? He and Livie had twenty years of raising children ahead of them. Dain's team had just been practice.

The thought that his kid would be anything like his team sent a shudder of fear through him. His arms tightened involuntarily on Livie.

Tucking his head down against her neck, he breathed in her scent, absorbed her presence, safe and sound against him. And just like it did every time he was near her, his cock began to firm against her ass, the adrenaline of the fight morphing into something far more satisfying as it pumped through his veins. "Think we could sneak out of here while the children are preoccupied?"

Livie's chuckle rubbed her body along his, pulling a groan from his chest. "Please."

"Your wish, wife…" He nipped the tender skin of her neck as he assessed his options. Unfortunately he couldn't go far—they would be forced to stick around and give statements sometime in the next couple of hours, no doubt. But he could go far enough to give him some privacy with his wife. Settling her gently on the floor next to the gurney, he took her hand in his and led her over to her office.

"Dain?"

He raised a hand to ward off Jack's inquiry. A faint chuckle said his boss got the point.

"I don't have the key on me," Livie pointed out as they stopped in front of her door.

Dain grinned over his shoulder, already digging into his pocket. "That's okay; I do." Probing along the seam, he forced the hidden compartment open and retrieved a lock pick Kelly's goons and the local

PD hadn't found. When he pulled it out, Livie grinned.

"Always prepared." She shook her head. "You're better than a Boy Scout."

"That's because I'm no boy," he told her with a quirk of an eyebrow. And then he went to work. Seconds later they were stepping inside.

The closed door cut off the noise of the outer room, cocooning them in quiet and, for now, peace. Livie slumped against it, her eyelids drifting shut. Concern shafted his heart. "Hey."

Her pretty mismatched eyes opened, taking his breath just like they always did. She tilted her hips to bring their lower halves together. "Hey, husband."

The nickname tugged at the side of him that was more than a warrior with an adrenaline-fueled hard-on—the need to take care of her rose. He went to his knees before his wife. "Are you sure you're okay?"

"I'm with you, aren't I?"

The softly rounded plane between her hip bones created the perfect cushion for his cheek. "And our baby?" The word caught in his throat. He wasn't sure how long it would take to say it without a hitch, but he didn't care. The awe of the gift Livie was giving him couldn't be hidden behind macho bullshit.

She cupped his face and pressed him into her. "We are fine, both of us. I'm not even nauseated anymore."

A lightbulb went off in his brain. "That's why you were up this morning, wasn't it?"

"Maybe."

He turned his head to look up at her, eyes narrowed. "Livie…"

"Dain." Her smile was sweet, patient. He wanted to kiss it away, right after he spanked her for not telling him what was going on.

Shit. Could he still spank her if she was pregnant?

"I don't really want to talk, okay?" she was saying as his mind raced. "I just had my life—and yours, and our child's—flash before my eyes more than once. I'd like to do something that would affirm that life a bit; wouldn't you?"

Dain set aside the spanking issue as hunger flared deep in his gut. Livie's request had given him permission to let go, and his body did, even if his mind wouldn't loosen the reins completely—she might want him, but there was a tired look in her eyes.

"I would," he agreed, standing. "Come here."

He led her to the small couch that took up one corner of her office. Her breath quickened as he drew off her shoes, her slacks, her panties. After laying her down, he unbuttoned her shirt and opened the front clasp of her bra. Livie lifted her hands to the armrest, the act stretching her body out like a sacrifice, all creamy, glowing skin against the deep blue of the suede couch. There was something sinful and so damn sexy about her firm breasts poking up between the sides of her silky shirt, the fact that she was half-clothed and he still had every stitch on. His gaze refused to leave her, so he backed slowly to the door without turning, fumbled for the handle, and flipped the lock on.

"Dain."

She reached for him, and he couldn't say no. His vest came off on the way, his belt. He had his fly open by the time he knelt next to the couch.

"You're so fucking beautiful," he whispered hoarsely.

"You say the sweetest things."

Her hands settled back above her head as he leaned over her. The rise and fall of her breasts quickened with her breath. Dain watched, mesmerized, for the longest moment before lowering his head to lick one hard berry-red nipple. He didn't touch her anywhere else, only that small nub, again and again, drawing out the moment and her hunger and his own. When Livie began arching up, begging without words for his sucking, he gave it to her.

The wail she muffled behind her hand was his reward.

His head swirled with raw lust and tenderness, the taste of her in his mouth and the pounding in his groin. He bit down lightly, holding her still, trapping her nipple in his mouth as he moved onto the couch to cover her. To tuck her beneath him and wrap his body around her and push their hips together until the creamy folds of her labia embraced his cock. Livie accepted all his weight, pulled him down harder between her parted knees. Bringing him home, where he belonged.

When his cockhead pushed against her opening, he shivered at the force of the pleasure soaring in his veins. The tight fit of her welcomed him, and he savored it, savored the wet clench gloving him inch by inch by inch. He pushed until their pelvises ground together and he couldn't get another centimeter inside her, and only then did he rise up to meet his beautiful wife's eyes.

"Livie, love—" The hoarse words begged to be said, but nothing else came. He put his tongue to good use by kissing her, letting his tongue speak the words his brain couldn't process with need pounding so hard inside it.

Livie tilted her hips, urging the base of his cock against her clit, and a shudder rocked her body. He knew that shudder, the one that came right before she went off. He knew everything about her, and yet it only excited him more, not less, even ten years later. Another time he might've backed off, made her wait, drawn out the moment, but neither one of them needed to wait today. They needed this, the connection, the mad rush of climax in their veins, if only to remind them what living was all about.

His wife. That's what it was all about.

So he pulled back, just far enough for Livie's fingernails to dig into his sides. The snap of his hips shoved him deep, his body pounding against her clit. A sigh of pure satisfaction passed from her lips to his. When her muscles clamped down hard, his eyes rolled back in his head.

"Hurry, Dain. Please hurry."

He did. The heavy thrusting, the hot slide of her around him drove him quietly insane—Livie too, if the strain in her expression was anything to go by. Needing her closer, needing everything he could get, he shoved his hands beneath her hips and forced her against him with every advance. It took less than a minute for both of them to tense, for their breathing to stop, for their bodies to detonate into a million tiny pieces, but it was still too long. And when the pieces came back together and Dain could savor the feel of Livie tucked under him, soft and warm and relaxed, all he wanted was to start back at the beginning and repeat the whole thing a couple hundred times. In fact…

A knock on the door stopped him before he could move. "Daddy! Kinda need you out here!"

Elliot.

Dain groaned into Livie's sweat-damp neck.

"Guess you gotta go, huh?" she murmured, her breath tickling his ear.

He didn't move. "*I'm* not going anywhere; you're coming with me."

"I am?"

"You are." He couldn't stand to be separated from her right now. Maybe ever. How they'd work that out with a baby, he didn't know, but Daddy had been here first, so he got dibs.

He shook his head at himself even as he squeezed down the slightest bit harder on Livie. His throat went tight. "One thing we need to get straight, wife."

"What's that?"

Another knock on the door. "Dain? Stop fucking around and get your ass out here." King.

"They've sent in reinforcements," Livie said, amused.

Dain ignored the door and lifted up to stare into her unusual eyes, trying to convey through the intensity of his look how goddamn much he needed her to understand his words, even if it took his best alpha-male commander bossiness. "Livie…don't ever hide something from me again. Don't. I need to know what's going on with you. Always, got it?" He didn't think he could live through this again, not without his heart stopping. He couldn't. He needed his wife and child safe and sound, always.

Livie smirked, just like she always did when he tried to boss her around and she had no intention of following "orders." How many times had he seen that look since they married? But this time he meant it.

When he said exactly that, she didn't get mad. Mutiny didn't make an appearance. Instead she rubbed her nose against his and stared into his eyes with green and brown innocence that instantly made him suspicious. "Yes, husband." A kiss, a reassurance. His cock jerked where it rested, still inside her warm depths. "I won't hide from you. But…there's nothing to hide now, is there?"

Chapter Twelve

Olivia laid her hand on Dain's bouncing knee. "Be still."

"Still? I'm still." He glanced at the thick black watch on his wrist, the kind his entire team wore, with more displays and buttons than she'd ever figure out how to read. The watch complemented the masculine sprinkle of black hair along his muscular arm, but today that arm was twitchy. Just like his knee.

She clamped down on the thick thigh muscle beneath her hand. "You are not."

"How much longer?"

"Not long." It better not be long. Her bladder already felt like an over-full balloon about to explode from the water they'd ordered her to drink. She had a feeling when they got into the exam room for the ultrasound, the organ would obscure any view of the baby they hoped to have. And that was if she managed not to wet the table while they ran the probe over her stomach.

Dain sat still for maybe thirty seconds before his leg started twitching again. Frustration began a slow rise in the back of Olivia's mind, but she refused to give it room to grow. Nothing was going to ruin this moment—not Dain's nerves, not her need to pee, nothing.

They both needed distracting, that was all.

"I'm surprised your team didn't show up." She wouldn't have put it past them. They really were like her and Dain's kids sometimes. Her lip quirked up.

Guess she wasn't a totally inexperienced mom after all—she had four grown kids to prove it.

"Mmm."

Gimme something to work with here, husband.

"So what's the pool up to now?" They had a running bet on the sex of the baby, though she didn't know who had voted on what.

"Five hundred."

Olivia choked, both from the number and from the sound of Saint's voice at her elbow. When had the damn door opened? "What are you all doing here?"

And it was all of them. Saint, King, and Elliot lined up like good little soldiers in the waiting room, staring down at her with mixed degrees of amusement. They even had their weapons strapped in place. What, did they think she might come under attack from the ultrasound tech?

She glanced at Dain. He didn't look surprised. She narrowed her eyes at him.

Dain shrugged.

Men.

She looked to Elliot, hoping for at least some spark of sanity there. "What are you all doing here?"

Elliot's brow creased. "Dain said you had an appointment." Like *obviously we'd be here.*

The pain in Olivia's bladder precluded following that line of thinking.

Saint's mind was back on the baby pool, apparently. "Five hundred as of this morning, but that's just us. The other teams have their own pools."

"Why would the other teams have pools?" She turned her back to Saint, unable to handle the full force of the entire team's stare at the moment. Dain was easier. "How did this happen?"

That distracted Dain enough to forget his nerves. He grinned and slanted her an arch look, the boyish expression at odds with the sprinkling of gray barely beginning to show in the stubble along his chin. He'd gotten out of their joint shower too late to shave this morning. "I'm a popular guy, you know."

"No doubt."

He opened his mouth, probably to say something about her sass. Elliot interrupted.

"Don't worry, Livie. Whoever wins, the money is going into the kid's college fund. We can't have our baby starting out life poor. I mean, look at his dad."

Olivia did. "'Our baby.'"

Dain had the grace to look the slightest bit sheepish. She turned to Elliot. "'His'?"

Elliot tilted her head, her gaze questioning. "You don't think he"—she nodded to Dain—"would throw a girl, do you? I mean, it's Dain."

He was all man, Olivia had to give the woman that. But she had a feeling Elliot wasn't as right as she thought she was. Call it mother's intuition, but…

Dain took exception to Elliot's assumption. "I'm man enough to 'throw' boys and girls, little Otter. And I'm not a horse, you know."

"That's what she said." Saint chuckled at his own pun. The rest of the group roared with laughter.

Olivia glanced at the inner office door and prayed someone would come rescue her before she sprang a leak.

The nurse chose that moment to poke her head out into the waiting room.

"Mrs. Brannan, we are ready for you. Would you and your husband like to come with me?"

Dain stood silently, his hand reaching for hers. For a moment she wasn't sure if he was trying to help her from her chair or looking for support himself. The clasp of their hands reminded her it didn't matter. This went both ways. They gave to each other, took from each other, and found themselves in their partner. And she'd thank God every day that Dain—and now this baby—gave her that. They belonged to her.

When the two of them stepped forward, so did the team.

"No, sorry." Olivia tried to smile, but she was suddenly too nervous for her lips to stretch that way. "You guys can wait here." No way did she want Dain's team witnessing her wetting the table. And if something was wrong... No, she needed just Dain, much as she loved the rest of them.

"We'll stand guard," Elliot assured her.

Do I need a guard? She looked to Dain, who winked at her on the side Elliot couldn't see.

"Mrs. Brannan?"

The nurse. Right.

Olivia followed her into a room much like the normal patient rooms, with a similar table to lie on and the same damn paper that stuck to her bare butt anytime she sat on it. She gave it a death stare before turning back to the nurse.

"We need you to hop up onto the table and pull your waistband down under your belly, please."

No bare butt? Relief eased her nerves until she realized that if she wet her pants, she'd have no clothes to go home in.

Dain helped her get settled. They had a few more minutes alone for their nerves to ramp up again before Maryann entered the room.

"You ready for this, girlfriend?" Maryann asked, settling onto the chair situated in front of the ultrasound machine.

"I think whether I am or not, we better get this show on the road. My bladder's about to bust."

Maryann chuckled. Dain squeezed her hand. When she met his eyes, amusement and tenderness and fear all warred in their depths. She squeezed back.

Maryann fiddled with settings and probes and bottles of warmed KY Jelly. The first swipe of the machine over her belly brought a groan from Olivia.

"Yep, your bladder's full," Maryann said. "Hold it in."

"That's easy for you to say."

Maryann winked, then went back to her focus on the screen. All Olivia could see was gray static around the sides and a black cone of nothing in the middle. Maryann moved the wand around and pushed and fiddled. Clicked keys and buttons. Olivia bit down on her lip, seriously beginning to fear for her clothing.

"There's the little bugger."

Dain's sharp inhalation of breath filled her ears. Of all the moments in her life that were burned into her brain—meeting Dain for the first time, their first night together, their wedding, the morning showers and late-night cuddling sessions, so many things that had touched her heart and soul and bonded her to this man in a way that could never be broken or matched—that single breath felt most important. Her Dain, her warrior, revealing his fear and awe over something neither one of them could control: another human being. Tears stung the backs of her eyes.

And then she focused on the screen.

Oh God. Oh…

"Dain?"

"I see it." His grip felt like it would crush her hand. "I see it."

Maryann showed them the baby's arms and legs, measured its head and spine, counted the heartbeats, and all the while, Dain stared, rapt, at the fuzzy black-and-white image. Olivia split her time between him and the screen, fascinated by both. And then…

"Well, that's interesting."

Dain leaned forward, his anxiety palpable. "What? What's wrong?"

"Nothing's wrong." Maryann stared intently at the screen. "Though I don't think I would've won if I bet on the sex of this baby."

A muffled "What?" Filtered through the door, and then it opened. Saint stumbled in first, followed by an intent Elliot and a somewhat embarrassed King who kept his gaze firmly averted from Olivia's belly. She swore she caught a faint touch of pink on the poor man's cheeks.

"What are you three doing in here?" Maryann demanded.

But Olivia found she really didn't care. In fact, at this moment, she realized it felt right to have Dain's "other" family with them. Besides, she thought seeing their faces when they heard her news might be even better than only seeing Dain's.

Dain made introductions. "Now, you were saying?"

Maryann looked to Olivia, who nodded. They shared a conspiratorial wink.

"I was saying the sex of the baby is interesting."

"Yes, it is," Dain practically growled.

From the look on her face, Maryann was enjoying this far too much. She lazily moved the wand over Olivia's belly again.

The tension stretched, a cord about to snap. Finally it did—or Dain did.

"And?"

Maryann giggled. "Dain, I hate to tell you this, but I am under strict instructions not to tell you what the sex is."

"What?"

Okay, that was more than a growl. Olivia giggled this time.

Dain turned on her. "Why did you tell her that?"

She shrugged. "I have to keep things interesting, don't I?"

Thunderclouds gathered in Dain's eyes. The team added their protests.

"You guys go around making bets on the sex of my child, and you think little ol' Olivia has no say in the matter, don't you?" She shook her head at them. "I have all the say. I'm the one in control, and I say I want the baby's college fund to be as big as it can get, so keep betting. You've got at least twelve more weeks."

Elliot was the first to laugh. It took the men a bit longer.

While the room was still in an uproar, Dain leaned over, his lips coming to rest a breath away from hers. She savored the feel of being overwhelmed by him, especially in this moment—even if the moment was a little more crowded than they'd planned. "Hey, husband."

Dain glared down at her, but she could see the sparkle of amusement mixed in. "Keeping things interesting, huh?"

"Right. Ten years, you know. A girl only has so many secrets." She tried to look mysterious and elusive, but knew she failed miserably. She could try all she wanted, but Dain was in the business of secrets. He always managed to ferret them out.

"You know I'll get the information from you one way or another, right?"

Of course she knew, which was why—

"But you can't get it out of me, Dain," Maryann interrupted.

Dain's eyes went wide. "She's not— You're not—"

"That's right. She's not telling me either." Just twelve more weeks. What was twelve weeks when she might not get to savor having a secret from Dain for another lifetime?

This was going to be fun.

Dain leaned very, very close. "You know I'm going to punish you when we get home, don't you?"

Excitement did a dance behind her too-full bladder—which she really needed to do something about. But first… "Of course I know. I was counting on it."

If Dain's kiss was anything to go by, the next few weeks were definitely going to be worth it, in every way.

∞

Did you enjoy COME FOR ME? If so, you can leave a review at your favorite retailer to tell other readers about the book. And thank you!

For news on Ella's new releases, free book opportunities, and more, sign up for her monthly newsletter at ellasheridanauthor.com.

Before you go...

Elliot has always been alone, even within her team. Now she'll face the ultimate threat to her survival:

DECEIVE ME
Southern Nights: Enigma 2

A lone-wolf warrior and the family man she doesn't dare pursue.

Elliot Smith has trained hard to live alone and work alone, even when it comes to her job as a security specialist for JCL Security. No relationships, no ties, except the one to the man who kidnapped and murdered her mother. She'll do anything to kill Martin Diako, the untouchable South African pirate king. When Deacon Walsh walks into her office, she finally sees a chance to do just that.

Deacon went from soldier to mercenary warrior to stay-at-home dad, and now his past is back to haunt him. Martin Diako, the father of the terrorist Deacon killed two years ago, is coming for revenge, and he has his sight set on Deacon's daughter. An heir for an heir. Deacon will do anything to protect her, even if it means asking for help. But the security team he's hired comes with an added complication: the only woman to interest him since his wife died.

Deacon always leads his team, and Elliot protects hers. They might have one chance at their enemy—if they can work together. Will their hunger for each other pull them together, or push them apart?

∞

"Overwhelming emotion and heart-racing excitement. *Deceive Me* is something special. Ella Sheridan's best book yet!"

— *Blogging by Liza*

Turn the page for an exclusive excerpt from
DECEIVE ME.

∞

DECEIVE ME

Chapter One

"I'm not a fucking nanny, Dain."

"Not with a mouth like that."

Elliot shot a deadly look Saint's way, but her team member shrugged it off. She seriously considered strangling the man with the crucifix he wore around his neck, but it wouldn't matter. Their boss would simply replace him with someone even more annoying just to get back at Elliot for the inconvenience. Instead she turned her back to the room and sought calm outside the floor-to-ceiling windows providing a perfect view of downtown Atlanta.

Okay, the calm came from avoiding the three amused sets of eyes behind her, but whatever.

The members of her team remained silent, though she could feel their stares burning into her back. Good men. She couldn't have asked for better. Dain Brannan, or Daddy as they sometimes called him, was the head of their particular team here at JCL Security, the one who took care of the rest of them. Saint, or Iggy—the six-two, massive warrior took personal exception to the use of his full name, Saint Ignatius Solorio—was the joker of the bunch, always saying what everyone was thinking but would never politely admit. He also had an encyclopedic knowledge of weapons that made him invaluable despite the constant temptation to kick his ass. And then there was King—Kingsley Moncrief. No one would guess from looking into the man's assessing eyes that he'd been raised with a silver spoon in his mouth. Acting as their client and media liaison was a natural role for him, but Elliot had never doubted how lethal King could be in the field.

All three men stayed quiet, waiting for her cool head to take over. Waiting for the pressure of their silence to push her into complying. They knew her as well as she knew them.

"I don't want to be shoved into a role because I have the requisite vagina," Elliot bit out.

When Dain chuckled, she whipped around to glare at him. He raised a hand to stop her in her tracks, a smile still on his lips. "Think about it, Otter. A four-year-old girl. Look at us." He gestured at the two men flanking him, both over six feet and muscular. Tough. Scary, if you weren't Elliot. "Do you really think a child is going to be particularly comfortable with us? Or that she'll trust us as fast as she needs to? This isn't some forty-year-old visiting dignitary's wife we can simply talk into complying; it's a kid."

Elliot refused to let Dain's use of her call sign influence her. "She would trust you. Everyone trusts you." And they did. Dain wasn't called Daddy only because he watched out for his team.

"Maybe. But with you, it's guaranteed."

Because she was tiny. The truth of the knowledge burned in her gut. She didn't like appearing weak, though she wasn't above using it to her advantage. She'd taken down many a fighter in the ring because they thought she was an easy target. They learned otherwise quickly, much to their detriment.

So yeah, she got it. That didn't mean she wanted to admit it.

Elliot sighed like a teenager being forced to wash dishes instead of a kick-ass security specialist being assigned a new client. "Do I really have a choice?"

No, of course not.

The side of Dain's mouth quirked up in a smirk she knew meant he thought he'd gotten his way. Again. Bastard. "Not really."

Another sigh. "Fine."

That earned an all-out laugh. "Fine. Can we meet the client now?"

Elliot grumbled under her breath as she followed Dain to the door of his office. King chuckled as he fell in line behind her. Saint, of course, simply had to add an, "And don't forget to watch your mouth, little Otter."

Elliot growled back at him before she stepped into the hall.

JCL Security was headed by Conlan James and Jack Quinn. Their reputation in the United States security community was unparalleled. Even Elliot had heard of them before Dain found her and convinced her to join his team two years ago. She respected her bosses, and Dain's influence on her life had been such that she'd do pretty much anything he asked, but he'd also never asked her to babysit children. She knew nothing about children. Even when she'd been a child, she hadn't been "normal," so how the hell— heck—was she supposed to understand how to handle a child? The mere thought had her wishing for a paper bag to hyperventilate into as their group came to the door of Jack Quinn's office.

Dain glanced over his shoulder, one last assessment of his "troops" before presenting them to his commanding officer. His gaze settled on Elliot, and the warmth she recognized there eased the panic in the pit of her stomach. When he nodded, she found herself squaring her shoulders and putting on her game face.

Dain gave a peremptory knock and opened the door.

Here we go.

Her gaze shot immediately to the head honcho's desk, but the sight of Jack was blocked by a set of wide shoulders wrapped in a tight black T-shirt. Wide, muscular shoulders. Elliot saw the same sight nearly every day—all of her team members were "built," so to speak; they all dressed in what she called military casual, fatigues and tight tees. None of them had ever made the breath catch in her throat like this man did.

Brown hair left shaggy at the top, cut close in a semimilitary style as it tapered to a cropped V at the base of his skull. Tanned skin along his neck and heavy arms. The man's back narrowed to a tight ass and legs that told her he was just as strong as Saint or King or Dain, so what did he need with them?

Oh, right. Kid.

Forcing herself to stop eating up his manly form with her eyes, Elliot fell into line next to Dain to one side of Jack's desk.

Their boss made the introductions, alpha to alpha. "Dain Brannan, this is Deacon Walsh."

Deacon? Actual name or military call sign? Their team all had call signs they went by while on mission, but clients typically didn't. There hadn't been time to brief them on more than the very basics of the assignment—number of clients, degree of threat. A call sign gave her a small hint as to why the guy looked like he'd be the last person asking for their help, though.

"Please, call me Dain." The two men shook hands, and that was where Elliot focused. On their clasped hands, not on the sudden uneasy squirm in her belly. She didn't understand what was wrong with her. She didn't question clients, and she sure as hell didn't have a…reaction…to them. But there was no doubt that everything feminine in her, all the parts she'd thought were good and dead, thank God, were doing weird dances in this man's presence. And she didn't like it. She didn't like it one fucking bit.

"Deacon, meet my team: Elliot Smith, Saint Solorio, King Moncrief. Elliot will be assigned to your daughter's personal protection, of course."

"No, she won't."

That jerked her head up. Her gaze clashed with grim brown eyes in a grim, hard face. Deacon Walsh stared down at her like she was a puppy who'd just pissed on his boot. "Excuse me?"

"I said, no you won't."

Dain shifted next to her. "Elliot is the best member of our team to—"

"You're not assigning your weakest guard to my daughter simply because she's a woman."

It had been Elliot's argument too, sort of, but instead of cheering, she gritted her teeth. Was this bastard saying she was too little to kick ass if she needed to?

She didn't even realize she'd tried to step forward until Dain's hand came out, blocking her advance. Elliot settled back on her heels and waited. Of course, she glared daggers into the man's stern eyes while she did it, but what were they gonna do, fire her?

The thought almost made her snort. She held back just in time.

"Mr. Walsh…"

Dain's words were cut off with an abrupt slash of Walsh's hand. "My daughter is top priority on this assignment. Nothing else matters but her. She needs more than one scrawny wom—"

"Did you just call me scrawny?"

Elliot felt more than saw her team members take a step back, Dain included. A warm rush of pride filled her at their acknowledgment that she could fight her own battles, but she didn't allow it to get in the way of her focus on Walsh. His gaze swept over her, and though she thought she detected a hint—a very vague hint—of embarrassment in their depths, mostly his eyes held frustration and anger. So did his response.

"I sure as hell did."

The final word was barely past his lips when Elliot struck. A fake palm heel to the big man's chin had him jerking back instinctively, giving her a mere second to connect a kick with his inner thigh. She did avoid the groin, though—no need to thoroughly piss off the client, after all. Her grin was probably a tad too exultant as the strike brought Walsh's head forward, right into her elbow.

"What the fuck!"

"Smith!"

Chuckles from her teammates mixed with Dain's and Jack's shouts as she grabbed Walsh's closest arm and turned, putting her back to his chest. When she dropped to one knee, Walsh flipped over her head. *Ah, the joys of leverage.* He hit the floor back first. A quick arch and push brought him to his feet—just in time for Elliot's swift kick in the ass. Walsh stumbled forward.

Dain caught him, fighting hard to keep the grin on his face under control.

No more than fifteen seconds had passed, but Elliot was already briskly brushing her hands together like she'd finished taking out the trash. Or proving a point. Said point might get her fired, but what the hell. They were used to her lack of communication skills around here.

Jack sputtered behind his desk, his face a shade of red she'd never seen on him before. Not very flattering.

A loud laugh pulled Elliot's focus to the client. Walsh bent, his back to her, the long furrow of his spine drawing her attention right down to the best ass she'd ever laid eyes on—and in her line of business, she'd laid eyes on a few. A warm hum that had nothing to do with a good fight sparked deep inside her.

Dain shook his head, one hand coming up to rub tiredly at his eyes. Elliot shot him a sheepish look.

Jack cleared his throat. "Mr. Walsh, I apologize—"

Walsh's raised hand precluded any apology. "No need, Jack." He turned, and Elliot read the amusement in his expression with relief. So maybe she wouldn't be fired today. "I believe I'm the one who should be saying those words. Nice job, Smith."

Not *Miss Smith*, which was what most clients labeled her with. Just Smith. As if she was one of the guys. The final bit of resentment fizzled out. *Okay, I can work with that.*

That was when she noticed the heat in her cheeks. Looking anywhere but at their client, her gaze met Saint's. When she moved to stand next to him, he leaned in to whisper, "Don't bother being embarrassed now, Otter. Too late."

She punched him in the ribs. His groan was covered by Dain clearing his throat.

"Let me assure you, Mr. Walsh"—Dain threw her a "we'll definitely talk about this later" look— "that Elliot will be much more circumspect with your daughter than she has proven to be here, won't you, Otter?"

If she said no, she might get out of the whole nanny duty thing, but one glance at Dain said she'd pushed as far as he would allow her to. She cleared her throat of rebellion. "Of course."

Walsh's gaze skimmed her before returning to Dain. "I have no doubt." He turned to Jack. "Now that we have that clear, perhaps we should get to the point."

"Right." Jack gestured them over to a conference area, where he, Walsh, and Dain took seats. Elliot stood next to Saint and King, lined up like good little soldiers behind Dain's seat, looking on as Jack opened a thick file on the coffee table before him and pushed it toward their team lead.

Dain planted his elbows on his knees and leaned forward over the intel. "Objective?"

"Protection," Walsh said before Jack could speak. "My daughter is the primary objective. Despite my performance here today"—Walsh didn't look her way, though his tone was filled with chagrin—"I don't need protection from this bastard. But I can't be with Sydney 24-7. I need someone who can."

"What bastard?" Dain asked.

Jack answered this time. "Martin Diako."

Elliot froze, even her breath stilling at the name. *Martin Diako.* She stared at the back of Dain's head, pinning her composure on her lifeline to the man who'd taken her under his wing.

Martin Diako. Fuck.

Deacon and Sydney Walsh needed protection from Martin Diako. The man known as Mansa in most circles. *Ruler.* The monster in charge of the biggest modern-day African pirating organization operating today. The monster responsible for ruining an untold amount of lives in the last forty years, including Elliot's own.

The monster who was her father.

**Pick up your copy of *DECEIVE ME*
at your favorite retailer now!**

∞

"I have a handful of authors that write books that I consider comfort reads. I can typically rely on these books to bring me joy when I'm in a reading slump. Ella Sheridan is one of those authors."

— *Blogging by Liza*

About the Author

Ella Sheridan never fails to take her readers to the dark edges of love and back again. Strong heroines are her signature, and her heroes span the gamut from hot rock stars to alpha bodyguards and everywhere in between. Ella never pulls her punches, and her unique combination of raw emotion, hot sex, and action leave her readers panting for the next release.

Born and raised in the Deep South, Ella writes romantic suspense, erotic romance, and hot BDSM contemporaries. Start anywhere—every book may be read as a standalone, or begin with book one in any series and watch the ties between the characters grow.

Connect with Ella at:

Ella's Website – ellasheridanauthor.com
Facebook – Ella Sheridan: Books and News
Twitter – @AuthorESheridan
Instagram – @AuthorESheridan
Pinterest – @AuthorESheridan
Bookbub – Ella Sheridan
E-mail – ella@ellasheridanauthor.com

∞

For news on Ella's new releases, free book opportunities, and more, sign up for her monthly newsletter at ellasheridanauthor.com.

41989705R00068

Made in the USA
Middletown, DE
13 April 2019